PROLOGUE

The horseman picked his way up the glen towards the crossroads. He felt bone-weary. The journey had been a long one. He was looking forward to a cool drink and a warm bed.

The softness of the Highland night wrapped around him like liquid silk. The rhythmic movements of the animal beneath him had lulled him almost to sleep. That, and the lateness of the hour – for it was almost midnight.

Not that you would have thought it from the lightness of the sky. Here in the far north of Scotland the summer nights never got much darker than dusk. Stars glimmered pinprick-pale against the translucent eggshell blue of the horizon. But on this particular night, there was no moon.

The month was on the cusp. The last sliver of the old moon had faded out the evening previous, the new one would not appear until the morrow. The world hung in astrological limbo, as though the very universe itself were holding its breath.

"Dark of the moon".

A night for hauntings. A pause between time and space. An unholy moment that allowed creatures of mythic evil to part the veil of their reality and slither through into ours. Or so the stories went.

There were those who would not venture out at dark of the moon, fearful of those wicked spirits let loose by the world's turning. Warlocks and waterhorses. Goblins and ghouls. And, worst of all, that dreaded guardian of the charnel house, the death Bogle. An amalgamation of all things foul. Known to lurk at crossroads – where malefactors were hung, suicides buried and witches burned – awaiting its chance to pounce on the unwary traveller.

Best not to tempt providence. Safer by far to stay indoors.

The horseman did not subscribe to such superstitious nonsense, of course. He was a pragmatic man. This was 1737 for heaven's sake, not the Dark Ages. And he a man of business. A factor, carrying land contracts from his master, the Earl of Argyll, to the Laird of Drumnadrochit. What did he care for spooks and spirits? Another hour and he would be at his destination.

Crossmaglen loomed ahead. He pulled on the bridle, drawing the tired mare to a halt, leaning forward to stroke her sweat-soaked neck in a gesture of encouragement and affection.

"Not long now, girl," he said. "If I'm no

mistaken Drumnadrochit should be over the next ridge."

The crossroads was in plain sight now, a small triangular patch of scutch grass where three stony paths met. Beside it, a huge basalt standing stone loomed against the skyline. At the very centre of the triangle stood a gibbet, the remains of what had once been a man dangling by the neck from its out-streched arm. A sudden breeze, blowing up from the valley floor, spun the corpse into an obscene dance, whistling through the fleshless bones, animating it like a puppet. The gallows creaked in mournful sympathy.

The mare started at the sound, eyes rolling as the breeze overloaded her sensitive nostrils with the carrion scent of decay. Her rider tried to soothe her, patting her flanks, calming her down.

"There, there, Bridie," he said. "Dinna fash yersel'. Tis but a poor loon, long dead. And the dead canna harm ye."

But this was dark of the moon. And the horse knew better. A sudden rustling sound from the direction of the standing stone threw her into a panic. She reared, almost unseating her master.

"Whoa, whoa," the horseman shouted, exhausted now, losing his patience. "What ails ye, ye silly brute? Stand still or I'll take the whip to ye."

And then his eye lit on the object that had spooked his mount, and a terror such as he'd never felt squeezed an icy claw around his thudding heart.

The "thing", whatever it was, stood motionless beside the standing stone from behind which it had emerged. Eight feet tall if it was an inch, fluid as mercury, it pulsed with a faint glow and exuded an atmosphere of utmost evil. Fern-fronds of mist formed and reformed around its insubstantial perimeter, while deep at its epicentre, occasionally visible, more often obscured, the horrified horseman thought he could glimpse a sea of writhing maggots.

"Who are you?" he gasped. "What are you? What do you want from me?"

But the spectre spoke not a word. Instead it edged silently forward, one long ectoplasmic tendril snaking out to grasp at the horse's bridle.

The animal took off, the man on her back clinging on for dear life, urging her far and away from the loathsome horror that followed behind. But the harder she galloped, the closer the creature came, moving ever nearer like an inescapable pestilence.

On and on they raced, up the mountain ridge, away from the pursuing nightmare. And then suddenly they could go no further. Above and in front of them a smooth granite rock-face rose to block the path. To either side, sheer cliffs fell away into nothingness.

The horseman slithered from the saddle,

scrabbling frantically for a handhold in the rock that would allow him to climb up to freedom.

But there was no way out.

He began to whimper, pleading with whatever fates might hear him for a means of escape, confessing his sins, begging forgiveness.

Not until he felt its icy breath on his neck did he at last turn and face his nemesis.

The monstrous apparition had stopped in its tracks, drinking in its victim's tangible fear, absorbing it into the swirling vortex of terror that was its very essence. Terror gleaned from the lost souls of former victims, long since dead. Savouring the moment, it bided its time, allowing the horseman to catch his labouring breath.

Then, from its formless depths a ghastly arm, livid as a drowned corpse, gradually took shape, stretching out a taloned claw towards its trapped and shivering prey.

The man's legs gave beneath him and he slid, back to the granite wall, into a hunker, raising his hands in supplication towards his tormentor.

"Please," he rasped, knowing even as he spoke that it was useless. "Spare me. I have a wife and child at home. For their sake ... for pity's sake ... let me go."

In reply, the creature leaned forward and laid one ghostly knuckle in the centre of the horseman's forehead. Then, with a blood-curdling howl of triumph, it swirled off down the mountain, the sound of its screeches echoing through the dark hills, causing those mortals still awake to pull the bedclothes over their heads or hold their loved ones just that little bit closer.

The horseman sat awhile in stunned silence. The night closed around him.

Down in the valley the flickering torches of Drumnadrochit spoke of a welcome and human company. Still he did not stir. What was the point? He was doomed and he knew it.

The Bogle, for he was sure this was what had confronted him, had laid the mark of death on him. Within a twelvemonth he would be as cold as the vile murderer swinging from the gibbet at Crossmaglen.

And he had heard enough of the legends to be sure that his would not be an easy passing. Rather it would be long-drawn-out and agonizing. Sweat-drenching fevers and bone-racking pain were how it started, the victim unable to eat, unwilling to sleep. All this exacerbated by the most soul-sucking dread imaginable. Sinking eventually into a dream-racked coma from which there was no escape. Daily becoming weaker, thinner, until all that was left was a bag of bones awaiting only the merciful release of the death-rattle.

And hanging over all, the baleful spectre of mortal fear.

The Bogle thrived on fear. Fear and anguish. Each gasp of agony was as meat and drink to it. Each painful spasm brought it a comparable ecstasy. Each moan or cry made it all the stronger. Word had it that when it had sucked enough souls dry it would be strong enough to break out of the confines now laid on it. No more dark of the moon. When it had fed off enough misery and distress, the Bogle would be unleashed to roam the earth at will, terrorizing helpless women, snatching innocent children from their beds.

The horseman pictured his own soon to be fatherless child, fast asleep at home, and his blood ran cold. Already he could feel a shortness of breath, a tightening band of steel around his chest. Nothing to look forward to then but a lingering death and the dishonour of having added fuel to the fire of a supernatural parasite.

Unless...

He raised his head. Why wait? Perhaps he might yet thwart the Bogle's evil intent?

Slowly, painfully, he dragged himself to his feet. Wrapping his arms around the mare's neck, he buried his face in her mane, taking a last crumb of comfort from the warmth of her quivering flesh against his clammy skin.

Then he stood back and slapped her hard on the rump.

"Off you go, girl," he said. "They'll know what to do with you."

He watched while the horse skittered down the ridge towards the lights of Drumnadrochit, her hooves striking sparks from the rocky outcrops, whinnying her terror into the night.

Not till she was out of sight did he turn towards the yawning drop that fell away beneath his feet.

When they found him, if they found him, old wives would shake their heads and purse their lips. More practical souls would assume he had lost his way and taken a wrong step as so many travellers had done before in these treacherous hills. Whatever, he would have done his duty. The vital papers would reach the laird. The land deal would go through. The earl would see that the factor's wife and child would not go hungry. And the Bogle would be confounded.

All that remained was to cheat that foul horror of its final triumph.

As the first rays of the sun inched above the horizon, streaking the new day with crimson and gold, the horseman stretched out his arms like a great wingless bird and, taking a single step forward, launched himself into the void.

1

The big, old house loomed out of the twilight like a crouching beast. Its shuttered windows looked blind as the eyes of a malevolent soothsayer. Its granite walls, grimy with neglect, gave off an air of grim desolation.

Peter's heart sank to his boots.

The place looked about as inviting as a mausoleum.

The red moving van, the only spot of colour in an otherwise grey landscape, was already parked in front, disgorging the contents of the cosy Hampstead flat on to the loose pebbles of the forecourt. A clutch of removal men scurried in and out like so many worker ants, sometimes singly, sometimes in pairs, depending on the size of the item they were carrying.

As they disappeared in through the great oak door, Peter couldn't rid himself of the notion that the house was eating the furniture alive. Swallowing it up as the men entered. Spitting them out like pips as they reappeared, arms empty, ready for another load.

It was as though they were feeding some gigantic alien monster whose appetite could never be satisfied.

His dad swung the car up the drive and parked it parallel to the van.

"Here we are," he said, cheerfully. "Home sweet home."

"It looks like something out of a horror movie."

Peter put all the withering disappointment and despair of the last three months into the statement. He hadn't wanted to leave London at all, his school, his friends, the bright lights of the city where he'd been born and bred. But Dad had insisted. They needed to be near his work on the North Sea oil rigs, he argued, so he could keep an eye on them. It would do them all good to get away from the memories.

"Who was the last tenant?" Peter said. "Dracula?"

In the back of the car, his younger brother, Johnny, began to cry quietly to himself.

"Have you no got sense at all?" hissed Mr Wilson. "As if he isn't upset enough, you've got to go scaring him to death."

"Don't blame me," said Peter. "You're the one who bought the house."

A figure emerged from the bowels of the building to stand on the front steps. A woman. Thin and spare as a stork. She was wearing a lovat green twinset and tweed skirt. Very old-fashioned. Mum had practically always been in jeans and a sweatshirt. And her blonde hair had been short and shiny, whereas this woman's was mousy and dull, pulled back in a french pleat that did nothing to soften the stern set of her features.

"Ah, Mrs McNab."

Peter's dad swung his long legs out of the car and scrunched over the granite chips to shake hands with his new housekeeper. She had come with the lease. A stipulation of the previous owner. It was an arrangement that suited Mr Wilson just fine. Where else would he find someone willing to take responsibility for two homesick boys and a large house in the wilds of the Scottish Highlands while he was offshore – which was more than he liked, and most of the time?

"The generator's on the blink," was her greeting to him. Her voice, clipped and curt, carried across to the car like a cold breeze. "Just as well there's plenty of candles in the house."

"The wicked witch of the west," said Peter, under his breath. "As soon as he leaves she'll probably lock us in the cellar and throw away the key."

Johnny let up a howl and flung himself face down on the BMW's upholstery.

"Shut up," said Peter, scornfully. "Don't be such a wimp."

"I miss Mum," sobbed Johnny.

"We all miss Mum," said Peter. "It's just that some of us don't make a song and dance about it. Be quiet. Here comes Dad."

Mark Wilson stuck his head through the open window.

"Come on, boys," he said. "Out. I've got to get to work. Mrs McNab'll get you settled in. What's the matter, Johnny?"

Johnny, face streaming, scrambled from the car and wrapped himself around his father's legs.

"Don't go, Dad," he pleaded. "Don't let her lock us in the cellar."

Mr Wilson shot his older son a furious glare.

"What've you been saying to him now?"

"Me? Why is it always me?" Peter grumbled, stepping out of the passenger side and facing his father defiantly across the car's flat roof.

"Because it always is," said his father. "Sometimes I just wish you'd remember that you're nearly sixteen and he's only six."

"Right. Six. Not six months. Not a baby."

"Oh, get inside," said his dad in disgust.

Peter mooched across the gravel to where Mrs McNab stood watching Johnny's histrionics with obvious disapproval. Mark Wilson unclamped his younger son from his leg and, casting a conciliatory glance in the housekeeper's direction, hunkered down to face him.

"Calm down, Johnny," he said, gently. "Nobody's going to lock you in the cellar. Mrs McNab's a very nice lady. She's going to look after you while I'm away. She's been working very hard to get the house ready for us. You wouldn't want her to think we didn't appreciate it, would you?"

Reluctantly, Johnny shook his head.

"Well then." Mr Wilson took a tissue from his jacket pocket and wiped the boy's face. "Besides, I'll only be gone a few days."

"You always say that."

"Well this time it's true. That's why I moved you up here, isn't it? So that I don't have to make the journey all the way down to London every time I have a weekend off? So I can spend more time with you? Anyway, Peter will be here."

"Peter doesn't like me."

"Of course he likes you. He's your brother."

"Then why's he so mean to me?"

Mark Wilson sighed. "It's part of being a teenager, I suppose. I'll speak to him. And I'll tell Mrs McNab to make sure he looks after you. Deal?"

Johnny gave a watery smile.

"Deal," he said.

"Come on in then," said his dad, putting an arm

round the boy's thin shoulders. "I'll get Mrs McNab to show you what's what."

Johnny allowed himself to be led across the forecourt to the steps where Peter already stood, scuffing his feet. But he held on tight to his dad's hand while Mr Wilson made the introductions.

"These are my sons," he said. "Peter and Johnny."

Mrs McNab nodded briefly and the two boys muttered their "hellos".

Johnny, still clinging to his father, stared forlornly up at the housekeeper's forbidding features. Her expression softened momentarily at the sight of his tear-stained face. Involuntarily she reached out to pat his head. Then, as if catching herself doing something shameful, she drew the hand back and wiped it on the side of her skirt.

Mark Wilson consulted his watch.

"I'd better be off," he said. "I'm sorry to throw you in at the deep end, Mrs McNab. But I'm late already. Time and helicopters wait for no man."

The housekeeper was suddenly all efficiency.

"You just get on about your business," she said, "and don't worry about a thing. The boys and I will be just fine."

"Thanks, I really appreciate it."

Mr Wilson, climbed into the car and stuck his head out the window. "I'm certain you'll get used to each other in no time. Mind you keep an eye on Johnny, Peter," he instructed. "I'm relying on you to look after him till I get back." He winked at his younger son. "I'll see you all at the weekend," he said and with a final cheery wave, he drove away, leaving the two boys standing disconsolately on the steps.

2

Mrs McNab allowed the BMW to disappear up the lane towards the main road before directing them indoors.

"Come away in," she said, "and let these men get on with their work. The sooner they finish, the sooner we'll be shot of them. You'll be wanting a drink, I suppose?" She made it sound more like an accusation than an invitation. "There's some tea brewing in the kitchen."

"I'd rather have a Coke," said Peter.

Mrs McNab raised her eyebrows.

"You'll have tea and like it," she said. "Coke indeed."

Then she turned on her heel and stalked off down the hall, the lining of her sensible skirt swishing against her shiny stockings.

Peter gave Johnny a nudge and the pair began to

follow her, though neither of them felt particularly enthusiastic about it. The interior of the house was even more gloomy than the outside. They looked with some trepidation at the long dim hallway. Heavy wood panelling and a threadbare carpet that had seen better days. As they padded past, they peered into the numerous unlit doorways that led off to either side, but it was too dark to make out much. Down at the end, a huge carved staircase rose to the shadowed recesses of the upper floors.

"I wonder if it's got a ghost?" whispered Peter, his voice almost obscured by the clump of Mrs McNab's heavy brogues.

Johnny sidled closer, taking Peter's hand, gripping it tightly.

"I don't like it here," he said in a loud whisper. "I want to go home."

"This *is* home," said Peter, brutally and then, seeing Johnny's face begin to crumple, he added. "I was only joking about the ghost. Relax. It'll probably look better in broad daylight."

But somehow, he had his doubts.

By the time the removal men had finished, leaving Mrs McNab to argue about their tip and tut over the mess they'd made and the dirt they'd tramped in, the sun was setting behind the hills and a mist, rising from the nearby river, was seeping into the overgrown garden.

Peter and Johnny sat silently in the cavernous kitchen with its flagstone floors and giant Aga cooker, munching on the sandwiches of brown bread and cold meat that constituted their supper.

Mrs McNab called them 'pieces'.

"I'll be back when you've finished," she told them. "I'll just go up and turn down your beds."

To Peter's enquiry as to where the TV was kept, she'd replied, "In the library. But there'll be no TV for the time being. Not till the new generator arrives. The old one's on its last legs. We daren't run anything off it right now except the lights. Luckily the hot water comes from the Aga, otherwise you might be washing in cold for the duration."

"When's the new generator due?" Peter wanted to know. Life without TV was an unheard of deprivation. What were they supposed to do? Play tiddly-winks?

"Not for a wee whiley yet," he was told. "Mr McTavish is having problems with one of the parts. If it doesnae arrive till the end of the summer, I'll no be surprised."

"The end of the summer?" Peter was aghast. "But it's only the middle of June."

"So it is. But what would you want to be watching TV for in the light nights anyway?" said the housekeeper, briskly. "When you could be out and about enjoying yourself?"

Peter took a gulp of his lukewarm milk and gazed glumly out into the gloaming. Out and about where, he thought? No cinemas, no cafés, no malls.

What on earth was he going to do with himself for the next three months? Stuck here, in the back of beyond, with his whinging younger brother and the housekeeper from Hell.

No TV. No video games. No computer. No hope.

"Are you cross at me, Peter?" Johnny looked up at his older brother under his long lashes. His big eyes were round as a frightened rabbit's in the half-dark.

"I'm not cross," said Peter, bluntly. "I'm just bored. And it's got nothing to do with you."

The summer stretched ahead, bleak and endless. Like a jail sentence. Not like summer holidays in London. In London, there was so much to do, there weren't enough hours in the day. Swimming. Football with his friends.

"Time for bed." Mrs McNab reappeared like a bad dream and ushered the boys out into the hallway, switching off the light as she went.

"Waste not, want not," she said, smugly, and stomped towards the stairs.

Away from the Aga's warmth, the building had a damp, unlived-in feel about it. Peter wrinkled his nose against the smell of mould and mothballs. He could just imagine mice nesting in the wainscoting. Or spiders skittering across the floorboards in the dead of night. He shivered. He hoped fervently that they didn't have rats. He doubted that he could deal with rats.

With its high ceilings and its draughty doorways

the place would cost a fortune to heat in the winter. Peter certainly hoped so. That way Dad might think better of it and move them somewhere civilized. Like Glasgow. Or Edinburgh. Even Aberdeen would be better than this.

He followed Mrs McNab's ramrod back up the wide oak staircase, Johnny trailing a step behind as usual. As they climbed, the housekeeper kept up a running commentary of regulations.

"Breakfast will be at eight sharp," she said. "Can't be shilly-shallying around till all hours with a house the size of this to run. I expect you to be down at the table by then. Washed and dressed mind. No nonsense like appearing in pyjamas. Dirty clothes are not to be left on the floor. I'm a housekeeper, not a skivvy. They go in the bins in the bathrooms. And no shoes in the house. I don't want mud traipsed in all over the carpets."

Behind her back Peter stuck out his tongue. Johnny giggled.

At the head of the stairs the housekeeper turned, fixing them with a stare. Peter assumed an innocent expression, like butter wouldn't melt. Johnny looked down at his feet.

"I'm not accustomed to having wains in the house," said Mrs McNab, frostily. "Mr Blane, the previous Master, wasnae married. Stick to the rules and we'll get along just fine. Otherwise..."

She left the word hanging in the air like a bad smell. Then she swung on her heel again and marched down the echoing landing, stopping about halfway along and pointing out two adjacent rooms.

"These are yours," she said. "Peter to the left. Johnny to the right. Your father will be in the master suite at the head of the hall. When he's home that is. You two can share the bathroom at the other end."

The rooms were as bleak and uninviting as the rest of the house. Full of shadows where nameless monsters, conjured up by vivid imaginations in the middle of the night, might squat, ready to leap out, fangs bared. All the better to eat you with, my dear. Dark recesses under the eaves made perfect hidey-holes for ghouls to crouch unseen, awaiting their chance to creep, sniggering, into your bed, the minute you closed your eyes. The only light came from the forty watt bulbs that swung from the centre of each high ceiling. Dimmed further by heavily-fringed brown shades, the glow they cast barely cut the gloom.

And the floorboards creaked.

Peter and Johnny looked at each other in ill-concealed dismay.

"Aye, well, things'll be cosier when you've got your own bitties about you," said Mrs McNab, breaking the silence. "I've put your suitcases by the bed. You can get unpacked and settled in, in your own time, in the morning."

As her one concession to homeliness, the housekeeper had placed Johnny's battered panda,

Fred, on his pillow by his pyjamas. He darted into his room to grab it now, rushing back out into the corridor as though pursued by demons.

"Where do you sleep?" he piped up, pulling at the housekeeper's skirt.

Mrs McNab looked scandalized.

"My rooms are on the top floor," she said. "Not that it's any of your business, young man. And, since I value my privacy above all things, I will thank you not, under any circumstances, to go up there unless you are invited." She turned a gimlet eye on Peter. "Either of you," she added. "Now get yourselves to bed like good boys. I'll be up in twenty minutes to put off the lights."

"But I always sleep with the light on," protested Johnny.

"A big laddie like you," Mrs McNab said, scornfully. "Time you grew out of such babyishness. The nights never get really dark here in the summer. You'll do just fine without."

Johnny's eyes scrunched shut and he opened his mouth to bawl.

"You can leave the light on on the landing," said Mrs McNab, grudgingly. "But only for the first few days, mind, till you get used to the place. We can't afford to put any strain whatever on the generator."

"Old bat," said Peter when she'd gone and Johnny had trudged miserably next door. "If she thinks I'm going to bed at nine-thirty in the evening she's got another think coming."

He reached into his carry-all and produced the lap-top his dad had bought him for his recent birthday. No party this year. Just the present. Mum had always arranged the parties...

"Peter."

Johnny stood in the doorway, in his nightclothes, clutching Fred to his chest. The buttons on his pyjama jacket were askew and his slippers were on the wrong feet. The belt on his dressing gown trailed forlornly behind him.

"What?"

"I don't like my room. It's dark and scary. Can I sleep with you tonight?"

"Are you kidding? Old bootface would probably go ballistic."

Stashing the computer under the bed, he stood up and ushered his younger brother back into his own room.

"Hop into bed," he said. "It'll look better when you get all your toys unpacked."

Johnny snuggled down, pulling the bedclothes under his chin.

"Can we do that tomorrow?" he said, sleepily.

Peter tucked him in.

"First thing after breakfast," he promised. "Now you go to sleep. And don't worry. I'm just next door if you need me."

"Will you come back and put the light back on after Mrs McNab's gone?"

Peter nodded.

Johnny sighed with relief and closed his eyes. "Thanks Peter," he said. "You're the best big brother anybody ever had."

Alone in his bedroom Peter had the good grace to feel guilty. He wasn't much of a big brother when all was said and done. He didn't have any patience with Johnny. Six year olds were a bit of a waste of space, in his opinion. Mum would have hugged him and laughed and told him he'd been six himself once and he should make allowances.

Easy for her to say.

He looked round the depressingly ugly room. That was another thing about Mum. She would have known how to brighten it up in two minutes flat.

"That's what mums are for," she used to tell them.

But then Mum wasn't here.

He sighed, forcing down the prickle behind his eyes.

Best not to think about that.

Instead, he fished the computer out from under the bed again and dug out his new game. He hadn't had a chance to try it out yet. As soon as Mrs McNab had come and gone he intended to have a go at it. Despite the long journey and the even longer day, he wasn't even remotely sleepy yet.

No sense in thrashing around awake for hours.

Anyway, what harm could it do? One little game. Mrs McWotsit would never know the difference.

Silly old trout.

Better just warm it up first though.

Peter plugged the machine into the ancient wall socket and turned it on.

And every light in the house went out.

3

Peter was in the doghouse.

Mrs McNab had left straight after breakfast, in search of an electrician to repair the generator. She was not pleased. When Peter had asked her why she didn't just phone the electrician and get him to come out, she'd said she couldn't because there was no phone.

No TV. No video. No computer. And now, no phone. Things were going from bad to worse.

As for the night before, he'd rather forget about that. It had ended in chaos. Johnny hurtling into his room, having hysterics, insisting on sleeping in his bed, refusing to be moved. Mrs McNab ranting and raving like a harpy. Totally over the top.

Unable to sleep for the heat and Johnny thrashing around, Peter had spent half the night sitting propped up on the window seat in a kind of semi-doze. He felt as though he hadn't slept a wink. Yet he must have nodded off because at one point – it had to have been in the early hours – he'd come to with a start, convinced that he was being watched. In that split second between sleep and waking, he'd been sure that there was something lurking out in the garden. A kind of a formless mist, hovering over the gate. But when he strained his eyes for a better look, whatever it was melted into the night. A trick of the half light. Or the workings of an over-active imagination. Whatever, in the daylight it all seemed very silly.

Peter yawned.

He'd be seeing UFOs next.

This morning he'd been exhausted. They all had. Johnny had been having nightmares again and Mrs McNab was like a bear with a sore head. At least she'd taken Johnny with her on the electrician hunt, which was a relief, but Peter had refused the offer of a lift into town, preferring to stay at home and mope.

"Suit yourself." Mrs McNab didn't try to persuade him. "Don't expect us back before tea time though. Johnny and I will probably have some lunch out."

Peter quite fancied some lunch out, but it was too late to back down. Mrs McNab and Johnny had driven off down the valley road to Drumnadrochit, five miles away, in her small red Beetle, and left him to his own devices.

He mooched round the house for a while poking

in nooks and crannies, looking for something to interest him, not finding anything. Each room was much like the next, panelled walls, high carved oak ceilings, big fireplaces, tall windows. Except for the library which was wall to wall books. Nothing readable, of course. Dusty, historical tomes, maps of the area, that sort of thing. Peter picked one out at random, flicking through the yellowing pages. A gruesome woodcut caught his eye. A woman tied to a stake, mouth open in an agonized scream as flames licked around her feet. Tiny pitchforked demons plucked at the long, dishevelled hair which framed a face of purest evil. Underneath, the legend read – "Jeannie McClure. Last witch to be burned in Scotland. 1737."

Peter replaced the book with a shudder and continued his tour.

The date over the front door said 1836, but the building felt older somehow, as though it had been constructed on the foundations of a more ancient structure. And there was no denying it, the place had a definite atmosphere. As if something infinitely nasty had happened there at one time or another. The cellar, leading down from the kitchen, smelt of damp and decay.

Just the place to bury a body.

The only area he didn't explore was the attic. Where Mrs McNab had her rooms. She'd wisely locked the door before she left, frustrating his intention of snooping around among her things.

After another half an hour he'd seen all there was to see inside. So he trailed out into the garden. Or what was left of it. The dry stone wall that marked out their plot of land was the only thing that distinguished it from the rough, heather-covered ground that stretched away to the horizon. A few clues remained to show there once had been order among the chaos. Some rose trees and a bird table, a greenhouse with a broken frame, a rusting lawnmower, a slime-covered carp pond and, right down at the far end, a stand of fruit trees, almost strangled now by the encroaching brambles. But otherwise the garden was as uncultivated as the rest of the valley.

Desolate.

Just like he felt.

He sat down disconsolately on the step outside the kitchen door, remembering the well-tended lawns round their flat in London, and how, in the summer, everyone would come out of the woodwork for barbecues and picnics. He thought of his mother's homemade lemonade. He thought of his mother.

He was just wondering, glumly, what on earth he was going to do with himself for the rest of the day, when the girl appeared from behind the greenhouse.

She was about the same age as himself – maybe a year younger – with wild red hair and a face full of freckles. She was dressed in grubby drill shorts held up with a piece of string and a khaki singlet. Her knees were scuffed and her lower legs criss-crossed with a fine tracery of bramble scars. She was barefoot and brown as a berry.

Peter thought she was a sight for sore eyes.

4

"I heard you were here," said the girl, by way of introducing herself, "so I thought I'd pop over and see for myself."

Her voice had the soft, sing-song lilt of the Highlands. She stuck out a grubby hand and looked directly at Peter with the greenest eyes he'd ever seen.

"Morag Sutherland," she said.

Peter shook hands solemnly. "Peter Wilson," he said. "Where did you spring from?"

Morag waved vaguely in the direction of the craggy hills.

"Thought you might need someone to show you the lie of the land," she said. "Are you on your own?"

"My dad's offshore. Mrs McNab and my younger brother have gone off to town for the day."

"Ah, Mrs McNab," said Morag darkly. "How are you finding Mrs McNab?"

"Miserable as sin and twice as nasty," said Peter. "But don't say I said so."

"I'm hardly likely to. Mrs McNab and I don't speak."

"Oh?"

"She doesn't approve of me. Thinks girls should wear skirts and knit jumpers. Got any wellies?"

Peter shook his head.

"Brogues then?"

"Come again?"

"Walking shoes." She indicated Peter's trainers with some disdain. "Those wouldn't take you the length of yourself round here. It's rough country. You'll need something stronger."

"But you're in your bare feet."

"I'm used to it. My feet have been hardened. You'll have soft, city feet, I'm thinking. The heather would cripple you."

"I've got some Doc Martens."

"They'll do. Go and fetch them. And bring something to drink while you're at it. We'll be gone for some time."

"Yes, sir." Peter gave a mock salute.

But he went all the same, returning ten minutes later with a bottle of Irn Bru and a couple of apples, one of which he handed to Morag. She polished it on the seat of her shorts before taking a huge bite.

"Let's be off then," she said with her mouth full.

And off they went.

Peter walked further that afternoon than he'd

cvci walked in his life. It wasn't that he was a couch potato, it was just that, in London, there was always a bus or a tube to take you wherever you were headed. In spite of himself he was impressed by the rugged grandeur of the scenery, the heather-covered slopes leading up over ever steeper paths to a point where only the rocks remained. By the time they came to a halt, at a crossroads where three paths met, his feet were killing him and he had a sneaking suspicion that there might be a blister or two forming on his heels. Also, he was famished.

"Where are we?" he said breathlessly, passing the Irn Bru over for Morag to take a swig.

She did so and then, digging in the pocket of her shorts, produced a package wrapped in greaseproof paper which, when she opened it, revealed two enormous cheese sandwiches, one of which she handed to Peter.

"Crossmaglen," she said as they both fell on the food. "Just look at that view. I bet you never saw anything like that in London."

Peter had to admit he hadn't. The great range of mountains, the towering peaks cut through with fertile valleys gouged out by retreating glaciers at the end of the ice-age, seemed almost untouched by human hand. No pylons. No TV aerials. Scarcely even a house. Halfway up one of the peaks, a small thatched steading, whitewashed mud walls glinting in the strong, pollution-free sunlight, clung to the mountainside like a limpet.

"Who on earth lives up there?" he said.

"That's the witchwoman's house," said Morag. "You don't want to be going anywhere near that. Not if you don't want a spell cast on you."

Peter hooted with laughter.

"Pull the other one," he said. "It's got bells on it."

Morag flushed red under her freckles.

"It's nothing to laugh about," she said. "Jeannie McClure has the second sight. AND the evil eye. You don't want to be messing with her. Her magic is very powerful."

"McClure? That's funny. I was just reading something about a Jeannie McClure in our library. Last witch burned in Scotland."

"Jeannie's great-great-great-grandmother," said Morag. "The line goes back for centuries. Burned alive," she added dramatically. "On the very spot that you're sitting on now."

Peter shifted uncomfortably.

"Gross," he said.

Morag pressed home her advantage.

"There used to be a gallows here at the crossroads. They'd hang people and then leave them to rot — or for the corbies to devour them. They say the first thing corbies go for is the eyes."

"Do you mind?" said Peter. "I'm eating. What's a corbie anyway?"

"A raven," said Morag. "You city folk don't know much, do you?"

"We know enough not to be scared by the evil eye, anyway," said Peter, bridling.

"Cross your fingers when you say that," said Morag. "Just to be on the safe side. They used to have human sacrifices here too, you know? In the old days. When the Druids were in charge."

"The Druids?"

"High Priests. Of the old Celtic religion. The standing stone behind you would have been part of a circle at one time. They used to build a giant wicker man and fill it with animals and people and burn them alive to ensure a good harvest."

"Charming."

"They passed on their secrets by word of mouth," said Morag, warming to her subject. "And if anyone betrayed them, do you know what they did?"

"No, but I have a feeling you're going to tell me."

"They flayed them alive and walled them up inside a tree and left them to die in agony."

"Look," said Peter. "Do you think we could change the subject? You're beginning to give me the creeps."

"Sorry," said Morag, standing up and dusting herself off. "I'm doing Celtic history for my special subject at school. I kind of get carried away. Where would you like to go now?"

"How far is it to Drumnadrochit?"

"Not far. About six or seven miles as the corbie flies. Do you want to go?"

She reached down and hauled Peter up beside her. He winced as he took the weight on his feet.

"I don't know that I'm up to it," he admitted.

"Maybe you're right. I shouldn't have taken you so far first time out. I'd better get you home."

"I don't want to go home yet."

Morag grinned at him. "Do you enjoy my company that much?"

"Course not," said Peter, the blood rushing to his face. "I mean, yes ... I mean ... it's just... This is the first time I've been shot of my brother Johnny for months and ... well ... you've obviously met Mrs McNab. What's to go home for? I'd rather have sore feet, thank you very much."

"You could come back with me, if you like. I can make us some tea and you can soak your blisters."

"Won't your mother mind?"

"My mother died when I was a bairn. I live with my dad. He's the local doctor. He's out on his rounds. He'll give you a lift when he gets back."

"Do you have a TV?"

"Of course we have a TV. What do you think, that we're savages?"

"Then lead on, Macduff." said Peter. "I'm right behind you."

5

In the event they never made it as far as Morag's. They hadn't gone more than half a mile (Peter having to stop every hundred metres or so to ease his now excruciating blisters) when a sudden mist came down. It enveloped both them and the mountain in a wet, white blanket that obscured everything in sight and deadened all sound.

"Hell's bells," said Morag, her voice muffled by the cloud cover. "This would happen."

"What? It's only fog."

"It's the haar," said Morag, flinging herself down by the side of the path. "You'd best take the weight off your feet. We could be here some time."

"What's the problem? I thought you knew the way."

"Like the back of my hand. But see for yourself.

You cannae hardly SEE your hand in front of you."

It was true. The haar, as Morag called it, was so dense that visibility was down to a couple of metres. And with the strange fog had come not only a penetrating cold, but a silence so palpable it almost hurt the ears. It was the kind of silence that made you want to hold your breath. Whisper rather than talk. Peter, accustomed to the constant thrum of city life, had never known a silence so intense. He didn't like it. He didn't like it at all.

"You mean we're stuck here?" he said, trying to keep the panic out of his voice.

"For the time being."

"So we're lost?"

"Not lost. But if we wander about in the fog we could GET lost. Or fall off a cliff. Or trip and break a leg and die of hypothermia."

"Don't be ridiculous. People don't die five miles from a town. This is the twenty-first century."

"And these are the Highlands. Rule number one about these mountains. If the haar comes down, stay put until it clears."

Peter eased himself down beside her.

"And how long is that likely to be?" he asked.

"Could be half an hour. Could be three days. Best preserve yourself in patience."

"Three days." Peter was horrified. "But it's freezing."

"Aye," Morag apologized. "That's my fault. I

should have thought to bring a jersey. But it didnae seem a likely day for it."

Peter had to admit that she was right. Half an hour ago he'd been worried about sunburn. Now he was worried about catching pneumonia.

"It'll get colder before it gets hotter," said Morag, as though reading his thoughts. "Once the sun goes down the temperature'll drop like a stone."

"Thanks," said Peter, sarcastically. "That's all I needed to hear."

"Cheer up," Morag grinned. "We can always huddle together for warmth."

"But surely somebody will come looking for us, won't they?"

"Not for a good whiley. Nobody knows where we are. I should have left a note for my father but I thought sure I'd be back well before him."

"What about Mrs McNab?"

"What about her? You didn't leave a note either. And knowing her, she'll probably be glad to be shot of you."

"Come on. She's not THAT bad."

"Don't you believe it. You know they say she did away with the last owner and buried him in the cellar?"

"You're kidding."

"All I know is that he disappeared one night at dark of the moon," said Morag dramatically, "and was never seen again."

"And my dad bought the house and kept her on knowing this?" Peter couldn't believe his ears.

"Nothing was ever proved. Anyway, he probably doesn't know the first thing about it," said Morag matter-of-factly. "The place has been on the market for yonks. The estate agent would hardly be likely to tell him."

Peter leaned forward and began to undo his laces. His feet had started to throb badly.

"What are you doing?" said Morag, sharply.

"Taking my boots off, what does it look like?"

"Well don't."

"Why not? My feet are killing me."

"Because they'll have swollen, that's why. If you take your boots off you'll never get them back on again. If we have to make a sudden dash for it, you'll be in trouble."

"Why should we have to make a sudden dash for it?" Peter tried not to sound alarmed, and failed miserably.

"With luck we won't have to. But there's snakes in the hills and wildcats and ... things."

"What things?"

"There used to be wolves. They died out in the twenties but they've been re-breeding them at the animal sanctuary over at Edenmouth, and a couple of them got loose last month."

"Great. So if I'm not frozen to death I'm likely to be eaten alive, is that it?"

"Don't exaggerate."

"I assume that's all. Or is there anything else I should worry about?"

"Well..." Morag hesitated. "There's the Bogle."

"The what'll?"

"The Bogle. It haunts these hills. But we should be all right. It only comes out at dark of the moon and that's not till next week."

Back in Hampstead, Peter would have laughed Morag to scorn. Even half an hour ago with the sun shining and the birds singing he would have thought the idea of something "haunting the hills" ridiculous. But now, shrouded in the cold embrace of the mist that even experienced mountaineers called the white death, he felt the hairs on the back of his neck prickle and goosebumps begin to form on his arms.

Then suddenly, from out of the silence, a long, low howl rose from the surrounding mountains. A sound fit to chill the blood. Like a werewolf on the prowl.

Peter nearly jumped out of his skin.

Morag turned towards him. Her green eyes seemed to have got bigger. But her voice, when she spoke, had only the slightest trace of a shake.

"Relax," she said. "It's probably just a sheepdog."

The sound came again, closer this time, a baying yowl, starting low in the throat and rising to a bloodcurdling crescendo before finally dying away into a silence prickly with tension.

Morag moved closer to Peter, reaching out to grip his hand. Her own was as cold and clammy as the sweat slicking his forehead.

"Then again, maybe not," she said.

Peter wished himself back at the house, swore he would never complain about it again, promised to be less grumpy with Johnny, to listen to his father, to do as he was told. Anything, just so's they'd get out of there alive. He imagined huge hounds circling in the mist. Tongues lolling. Serrated teeth dripping with saliva. Closing in for the kill. He'd said the house was like something out of a horror movie. But this was worse. This was like being in the middle of one.

The haar swirled around them like milky soup, tendrils forming and reforming like fractals on a computer screensaver. Peter strained his eyes, wanting, yet not wanting to see beyond the blind opaqueness that walled them in.

And then something moved within the whiteness. An insubstantial form, a grey shadow. Now you see it, now you don't. It loomed out of the cloud like a phantom, gliding silently towards them, bearing down. Upright, at least. Not a wolf then. But what?

The Bogle out on a haunt?

Peter was aware of a tall dark shape, cowled and hooded. Like death. All that was missing was the scythe. No features were visible but he could just picture the grinning skull lurking beneath the hood,

eyeless sockets agape and where the nose should be
– a big black hole.

He grabbed Morag in a bear hug, as though by
protecting her, he might better keep the thing at
bay. He could feel her heart thumping against his
chest, her breath rasping in his ear. His own heart
was beating nineteen to the dozen.

The figure advanced. Closer, closer, closer.

Finally it stopped, the heavy black material of
the cloak settling into the heather less than a metre
away.

Then it spoke.

"You two look as though you could be doing with
a lift home." it said.

"Jeannie."

Morag sprang to her feet, knocking Peter
sprawling. She flung herself at the figure, wrapping
her arms around it in relief.

"Am I glad to see you!" she said.

The hood fell away. Beneath it was, not the
anticipated death's head, but a woman's face framed
in a cascade of wild, black hair. Peter had a sudden
flash of the face in the woodcut, demons dancing
round the corscrew curls. Just a flash. Then long,
scarlet-tipped fingers appeared from the depths of
the heavy wool cloak to detach Morag gently and
pull the hood back in place.

"The van is just over the hill," said the woman,
her voice soft and soothing as warm chocolate. "I'll
just away and get it."

And turning, she disappeared the way she had come, the white wall closing around her like smoke.

"Dinnae move," the voice echoed back out of the fog. "I'll be right back."

"How come she doesn't get lost?" asked Peter, lightheaded with relief.

Morag looked at him gleefully.

"Because she's got special powers, of course. The wind and water at her command."

"And the haar?"

"And the haar. That's Jeannie McClure."

"The witchwoman. She saw us in her crystal ball and came to rescue us, is that it?" said Peter, picking himself up and dusting himself off.

"I wouldn't be surprised."

"Do me a favour."

"Why can't you just be grateful?" said Morag, hotly. "Why do you have to pour scorn on everything ... you ... you Sassenach! Think yourself lucky you were with me. Otherwise she might have left you here to freeze to death."

6

Peter was in the doghouse AGAIN. Only this time it was worse. This time his feet hurt as well.

The night before, Jeannie had dropped him at the gate, saying that she would need to get Morag home as soon as possible as her father would be worried about her. So he was left to fend for himself as far as facing the formidable Mrs McNab was concerned.

It was gone eleven when he let himself in the front door. The housekeeper descended on him like a ton of bricks.

He hadn't had a proper look at Jeannie McClure. When she came back with the van she'd still had the hood drawn back up over her head and, perched in the back, he'd only caught the occasional glimpse of her eyes in the rear view mirror. But she hadn't seemed particularly witch-like to him.

Mrs McNab was something else altogether. She bore down the hall on him like a raging madwoman, dressing gown flying, hair standing on end, candle held aloft in a hand shaking with fury. If she'd been riding a broomstick he wouldn't have been a bit surprised.

How dare he scare the life out of her, she had demanded, where on earth had he been? She had just been about to get dressed and get Johnny out of bed and drive back into Drumnadrochit to alert the mountain rescue team. Had he no sense of responsibility? Had he no consideration for anybody but himself? And on and on and on.

Not a word of concern for his ordeal on the mountain. No modicum of relief that he had emerged from the jaws of death unscathed. Just a tirade of abuse.

Peter, thinking about the body in the cellar, had backed up against the wall, apologizing profusely, explaining about Morag and the haar and Jeannie McClure.

"Morag Sutherland, is it?" said Mrs McNab, bitterly. "I might have known it. That young lady is no better than she might be. And as for Jeannie McClure..." she left the sentence trailing – as if words failed her.

Peter had finally managed to ease his way past her and hobble up the stairs.

"Don't think this is the end of the matter," she called after him. "It's not. Not by a long chalk. Your father will hear about this when he comes home. Until then you're not to see Morag Sutherland or to go out anywhere without telling me first."

As it was, she needn't have worried. The state his feet were in, he wasn't able to go anywhere. When he woke, they were throbbing fit to beat the band and had swollen to alarming proportions. He couldn't bear to put any weight on them and sent Johnny down to ask Mrs McNab whether he could please have his breakfast in bed?

Mrs McNab called it his "comeuppance" and sent a message back that he was not to be such a big jessie and to get down to the table straight away if he didn't want to go hungry. But even she was alarmed when he hobbled into the kitchen and she saw the size of his blisters.

"It's into the doctor for you, laddie," she said, suddenly practical. "You're in my charge and I'll no have people saying I didn't look after you properly."

The weather had turned wet and Peter felt like a complete idiot staggering to the car through the pouring rain in his flip-flops. But there was no way he could get his feet into socks, let alone shoes.

"I thought this was supposed to be summer," he said gloomily, as they drove down the narrow, twisty road towards Drumnadrochit. The cloud cover seemed low enough to scrape the car roof and Mrs McNab had to turn the lights on to see the way. The twin beams barely cut through the downpour.

"The weather's aye fickle in the Highlands," said

Mrs McNab. "I would have thought you'd have gathered that from yesterday's performance. I've driven down this road in sleet on the fourth of July." And then – ever the optimist – "Looks like it's on for the day."

"I'm cold." Johnny, shivering in the back seat, looked thoroughly miserable. He'd spent a bad night and it showed. The electrician was away doing some big job on a farm and wouldn't be back to see to their generator for another couple of days, so he'd had to go to bed with only a nightlight for company. Mrs McNab wouldn't hear of letting him stay up until his brother came home and what with worrying about whether Peter might suddenly disappear and not come back – like his mother had done on the day of the accident – and being terrified of imaginary monsters under the bed, he'd hardly slept a wink. And when he did eventually drop off, he had nightmares – about an evil grey something that had swallowed him up. He'd been lost in its centre and he couldn't see and he couldn't get out. He'd woken screaming in a cold sweat.

He'd got scant sympathy from the housekeeper then – and he got none now.

"You city folk," she said. "You'd think a bit of rain would melt you."

At least the doctor was less dismissive.

"That child looks half frozen," he said, when his plump receptionist had ushered them into the surgery. "Mary, make him a cup of hot chocolate and Mrs McNab will take a cup of tea while I see the patient. Now come on in Peter, and let's have a look at those feet."

Dr Sutherland chatted as though they were old friends while he sterilized and bandaged Peter's blisters.

"It's a pity you didn't make it over last evening," he said. "I could have caught them before they got into this state. You'd better stay off them now for a couple of days. Morag'll be disappointed," he added with a grin. "She was hoping to come and collect you this afternoon."

But his grin changed to a grimace when Peter informed him that he'd been forbidden to see Morag.

"Mrs McNab says she's a bad influence."

"Does she indeed? And what does your father say?"

"He's not here, is he? Anyway, she says she's going to tell him I didn't come in till eleven last night, so I don't suppose I'll be in his good books when he does get back."

"You don't want to worry too much about Mrs McNab," said the doctor. "Her bark is worse than her bite."

"Her bark's bad enough."

"Aye, well, maybe she is a bit sharp-tongued at that. It comes from not having a family of her own, poor soul. Put it down to being crossed in love." He patted Peter's ankle. "There, that should do you," he said, reaching for his prescription pad. "I'll give you a note for some painkillers and a jar of germolene. Ask Mrs McNab to come in, would you? I'll need to tell her about changing the dressings."

The reception area was empty when Peter went out. Except for the housekeeper, who was engrossed in the agony column of some dog-eared old magazine. Of Johnny there was no sign. But he could hear laughter and chat coming from the kitchen area at the back.

"She's filling him full of bicuits," said Mrs McNab in disgust. "I told her it would spoil his lunch but you might as well talk to the wall."

"The doctor wants to see you."

"Oh?"

"Something about the dressings."

The housekeeper rose with the air of a woman whose patience was sorely tried.

"As though I didn't have enough on my plate," she said, and stomped into the surgery.

"Come in, Mrs McNab," said the doctor, pulling the door to behind her.

Whether he left it slightly ajar on purpose, or whether it was a genuine mistake, Peter wasn't sure. Whatever, the sound of their conversation filtered out through the crack. Peter sidled closer so he could hear.

"I understand you don't think my daughter's good enough for your new charge?"

"Who told you that?"

"Let's just say I heard."

"Well, since you've heard, yes, I DON'T think she's suitable company for him. He didn't get back until gone eleven last night. What were they up to, the pair of them, until that hour? I was worried sick. I thought the Bogle might have got him."

"Oh, don't talk nonsense, woman. They were stuck on the mountain, that's where they were. The haar has trapped more experienced men than him in its time. You should be pleased that he got back safe and sound."

"Yes, well, if it wasn't for your daughter he wouldn't have been in danger in the first place."

"She knows that and she's sorry. At least she had the sense to stay put until help came."

"If you wish to let your daughter roam the countryside like a vagrant and stay up to all hours that's your own affair," sniffed the housekeeper. "But she's not going to lead Peter astray. Not if I have any say in the matter."

"I don't know what century you're living in, Mrs McNab, but the days of children being seen and not heard are long gone. And a good thing too. Where's the virtue of having them in bed by nine o'clock when the nights are light? If they had to get up for school I'd understand it. Otherwise what's the point? They'll go to bed when they're tired."

"They'll go to bed when I say so. I'm responsible for those two boys while their father's away. And I intend to do my duty by them."

"Even if it kills them, eh?"

"What do you mean by that?"

"Well, one of them's half crippled and the other one looks in dire need of a good cuddle. Draw your own conclusions."

"I don't have to stand here and listen to this." Mrs McNab swept out of the surgery, almost knocking Peter down in the process. "Mary," she shouted. "We're leaving. I'll thank you to bring that child out here. I haven't got all day to stand around while he stuffs his face with biscuits."

As they all piled into the car, the doctor appeared in the doorway and raised a hand in farewell.

"I'll have Morag pop round later and see how you're doing," he called to Peter.

Mrs McNab glowered through the windscreen, clashed the gears and took off down the road like a bat out of hell.

"What's got into her?" asked his receptionist, as he turned to come out of the rain.

The doctor shook his head.

"Poor wains," he observed. "Heaven knows I try to give everybody the benefit of the doubt. But sometimes I think Fiona McNab is just naturally a bad-tempered old biddy."

"If that's all she is they'll be lucky," said the receptionist, knowingly, closing the door on the downpour.

7

They were finishing supper when Morag turned up. Dr Sutherland had brought her over in the car on his way to a call-out.

"She's just come to see how Peter is," he called cheerily, when Mrs McNab opened the door, "and to bring a couple of bikes for the boys. There's an old one of mine that I never use that Peter can have, and one that Morag's grown out of that should suit Johnny down to the ground. They were just gathering dust in the garage. Might as well get some use out of them."

As he was speaking Morag was hauling the bikes out of the boot. Johnny, darting from behind the housekeeper's skirts, ran down the path to pick up the smaller one.

"I'm Johnny," he said, looking up solemnly at the red-headed girl. "I can't ride a bike yet."

"Morag," said Morag. "And you'll soon learn."

"I said she could stay for half an hour while I'm at the Lachlans'. I hope that's all right?" said the doctor.

Mrs McNab was about to say that it certainly WASN'T all right and why couldn't he bring his blessed bikes round at some civilized hour, but the doctor put the car into gear and drove off before she could make any objection. Morag grinned at the infuriated housekeeper.

"How's the patient?" she asked.

"He's getting on fine," sniffed Mrs McNab. "No thanks to you."

"So he'll be coming out then, will he?"

"No, he most certainly will not. I told your father before Morag Sutherland, and I'm telling you now, you're not welcome here."

"But Daddy said..."

"I don't care WHAT Daddy said, miss. Your Daddy's not the authority in this house. I am. And I say Peter is not going out."

"Hello Morag." Peter limped up to the door. It'd taken him all this time to make his way from the kitchen. "What're you doing here?"

"Came to bring you a bike. And to see if you'd like to come out for a bit. But Mrs McNab says no."

"Don't I get a choice in the matter?" Peter wanted to know.

"Not in this instance. I know best. If you haven't

the sense you were born with then I must have it for you. What's the point in my going to all the trouble of changing your dressings if you won't help yourself by resting your feet? Besides, it's past nine o'clock. Time you were both up in your rooms."

"Well, can I come in for a while then?" Morag was not to be intimidated. "That can't do his feet any harm, surely?"

"Of course you can," said Peter, before Mrs McNab could say no. "Come on into the library."

"Can I come too?" Johnny pleaded. "If I promise not to get in the way?"

"I thought Mrs McNab said it was your bedtime?" said Peter.

Johnny took the housekeeper's hand and looked up at her with soulful eyes.

"Please, Mrs McNab. Can I?"

"You can have as long as it takes for me to wash up the dishes," said Mrs McNab, grudgingly. "No more. This is another thing your father is going to hear about Peter. Heaven knows I only have your best interests at heart. But if my orders are to be constantly ignored then I'll have to ask him to find himself another housekeeper."

"I wish," said Peter, under his breath and Morag giggled.

"I don't know what you're laughing at, madam," said Mrs McNab. "Or what your father's thinking about, letting you out, on your own, at this time of the night. And it nearly dark of the moon..." and she swept off into the kitchen in a fret.

"Take no notice of her," said Morag, when the three of them were safely ensconced in the library. "Her bark is worse than her bite."

"That's what your father said," said Peter. "I just wish she wouldn't bark all the time."

"What did she mean about you being out at dark of the moon?" asked Johnny nervously.

Morag raised her eyebrows at Peter. He shook his head to indicate that she shouldn't mention the Bogle, whatever it was.

"Oh, it's just fairy tales." Morag reassured him. "The night between the old moon and the new moon is supposed to be bad luck. Spirits are supposed to be out. Silly superstition."

"And is this dark of the moon?" Johnny edged closer to Peter on the dark plush sofa. Outside the sun was going down and the library, never the cheeriest place at the best of times, was beginning to take on a sinister feel.

"No, it's a couple of nights off yet," said Morag. "Besides, you've no need to worry. As long as you're tucked up in bed you're safe enough. It's only if you're out and about."

"Bedtime, Johnny." Mrs McNab stood in the doorway, drying her hands on a tartan tea towel. "And don't you get yourself settled, missy," she said to Morag. "As soon as your father comes back you'll be out of here."

"He'll be ages yet," said Morag, after the housekeeper had ushered a reluctant Johnny out. "Mrs Lachlan's gone into labour. It's her sixth and she always takes her time. How're the feet, anyway?"

"Not great."

"At least they're on the mend," said Morag. "And by tomorrow you'll be able to ride a bike."

"That's true. If old bootface will let me out."

"She cannae very well prevent you."

"You don't know her."

"That's where you're wrong. I know her all too well."

"Why does she dislike you so much? What did you ever do to her?"

"Och, she's never forgiven my Dad for sacking her."

"Sacking her? For what? Stealing the family silver?"

"Nothing so dramatic. He hired her to look after me when my mother died but he didn't like the way she went about it."

"Can't say I blame him," said Peter.

"Aye, well, it was after that that she came up here to the big house to work for Mr Blane. He was an incomer."

"A what?"

"Like you. He wasn't from around here."

"And what brought him to this neck of the woods?" Peter's tone suggested that he couldn't imagine why anyone would move here voluntarily.

57

"He was a writer. Liked the quiet. And he was doing some sort of psychical research into mythical monsters."

"Like the Bogle?"

"That sort of thing."

She stood and wandered over to one of the bookshelves, running a finger along the leather bound spines.

"He had a great collection of books anyway," she said. "I'd love to borrow some of them. For my special subject."

Peter hobbled over to join her, squinting at the titles in the fading light, picking out the one he'd flicked throught the previous day. Leafing through the yellowing pages, he found the woodcut and handed it to Morag.

Morag took the book and studied the illustration. The flames, the demons, the woman's anguished face.

It might just have been Peter's imagination but the temperature in the room seemed to drop suddenly. Morag must have felt it too for she shivered, paling slightly under her tan.

"The likeness is uncanny," she said. "It could BE Jeannie."

"Well, it IS her great–great–great–grandmother," said Peter. "Take it with you, why don't you? She might like to have a look at it next time you see her."

"What about old bootface, as you call her?"

"I'm not going to tell her, are you?"

"I'd say the chances were slim to none," Morag grinned, stuffing the book up her jumper.

"I'll speak to my dad at the weekend," Peter promised. "See whether you can come over and work on stuff here. I'm sure he wouldn't mind."

"That would be great."

"Call it a return favour for the bike."

"It's getting really creepy in here," said Morag. "Do you think we could have the lights on?"

"The generator's bust," said Peter. "Sorry. But there's a couple of candles and some matches about somewhere."

He felt along the top of the mantelpiece, found what he was looking for, lit one and handed it to Morag then lit a second for himself. The dim flames cast an eerie glow up the walls and over the ancient volumes.

"Look," said Morag, moving to a corner cabinet. "There's some stuff by the man himself in here." She squinted through the glass fronted door. " 'Myth and Magic in Modern Times' by Hunter S. Blane," she read. "And two more — 'Ancient Beliefs – the Origin of the Monster', and 'The Way of the Wicca'. He was really into this stuff."

She tugged the cabinet door.

"Locked," she said. "Now why would that be?"

"Did you know him?" Peter asked.

"Only to see. I was only nine when he

disappeared. Tall man. Glasses. Stoop. Looked liked he'd slept in his clothes. Kept himself to himself mostly ... except..."

"Except?" Peter prompted.

"He came to the house one night. Very late. Claiming that someone was poisoning him."

"Who?"

"I don't know. The doorbell woke me up and I listened through the bannister, but I was half asleep, so I only caught part of the conversation. My dad gave him some indigestion tablets and told him to come round in the morning if he wasn't feeling better."

"And did he?"

"Hardly. That was the night he disappeared."

Peter lowered his voice. "And you think she did it?"

"I wouldn't put it past her. She used to scare the daylights out of me when I was young, saying the Bogle would get me if I didn't behave. I used to get terrible nightmares. My dad caught her at it one night. That's why he sacked her."

"Yes, but there's a bit of a difference between scaring someone to death and actually doing the deed."

"True. And it was probably only talk. People said she did it for spite. Apparently she thought he was going to marry her, started behaving like the lady of the manor, put a lot of people's backs up. Then all of a sudden he put the house on the market; said he'd finished his work here and was off to Borneo to do a thesis on witchdoctors."

"But he never got there?"

"No. He went out one evening at dark of the moon and that was the last anyone ever saw of him. Mrs McNab said the Bogle had taken him – but of course nobody believed her."

"What about you?"

Morag shrugged.

"So you think she poisoned him and buried him in the cellar?" Peter thought how, the first time – the only time – he'd been down there, it had seemed like the perfect place to bury a body. "How could she get away with it?"

"It was the middle of winter. There was a heavy snowfall that night. In the morning it was two metres deep. The police said he'd probably got lost and fallen down a crevice." She paused. "But they never found his remains."

"What are you doing with those books?"

Mrs McNab's icy voice cut the air like a hatchet.

Peter and Morag both jumped like scalded cats, whirling guiltily towards the sound.

The housekeeper stood in the doorway like a bird of prey, an old hurricane lamp held aloft in her right hand. The shadows cast by the guttering mantle threw the bones of her face into sharp relief, giving her already pinched features an evil, sepulchral air. The wide sleeves of her dark robe hung from her thin shoulders like a raven's wings.

With her beak-like nose and her black beady eyes she looked like nothing so much as those carnivorous corbies that hung around the crossroads waiting for something to die.

Peter wondered how long she had been standing there, how much of their conversation she had heard? Instinctively he backed up against the bookshelf, dislodging several volumes which clattered to the floor at his feet. One particularly old book split a seam on impact, scattering pages like confetti on to the carpet.

Mrs McNab bore down on them like the angel of death.

"Vandals," she hissed. "Those were Mr Blane's books. You have no right to touch them."

The sound of a car turning into the drive halted her in her tracks.

"That'll be my dad," said Morag, scooting past her. "See you tomorrow, Peter."

"Not if I see you first," said the housekeeper, following her into the hall. "Clear up that mess, Peter." She threw the order over her shoulder as she swept out. "And then get to your bed. We'll talk about this in the morning."

8

In fact they didn't talk about it in the morning. Quite the reverse. Mrs McNab didn't talk to him at all. She behaved as though he simply didn't exist.

When he came down for breakfast she stared at him, stony-faced, plonked his food in front of him and then proceeded to ignore him entirely.

This went on all morning with the housekeeper communicating, when she had to, through Johnny.

"Tell your brother it's time he had his dressings changed," – that sort of thing.

But Peter could feel her eyes following him everywhere he went.

He also noticed that she'd put a lock on the cellar door.

Eventually, round about noon, Morag rolled up on her bicycle to see if they wanted to go for a spin. Mrs McNab sent her away with a flea in her ear.

Johnny couldn't ride yet, she said and Peter was in no fit state to.

At tea-time, a message arrived, via the local postmistress, that Mr Wilson wouldn't be home for the weekend after all. He'd been called away at short notice to do some troubleshooting on a rig in South America.

This was par for the course as far as Peter was concerned, but Johnny was very upset.

"But he promised," he wailed. "He promised."

"Yes, well, circumstances alter cases," Mrs McNab told him. "A man's work maun come first. For sure he'll be back when he can."

"When he can be bothered," Peter thought. He'd wanted his father home so he could talk about the body in the cellar. Now it looked as though he wasn't going to get the chance.

He spent what was left of the day trying to teach Johnny to ride his bike, with little success. And then, just before bedtime, Morag re-materialized, this time with an invitation from her father that they should all come to Sunday lunch.

"Your dad can bring you over in the car," she said. "We're having chicken."

"Oh goody," said Johnny. "I love chicken," and then, remembering, "but Dad isn't coming home."

"Mrs McNab can bring you then," Morag grinned down into his distraught little face. "She's invited too."

"Tell your father thank you, but no thank you,"

sniffed the housekeeper. "I've a hundred and one things that need doing."

"But Mrs McNab," said Johnny. "I love chicken, I really do." He took her hand and gave her his most persuasive smile. The one that never failed. "Please. Can we? Please?"

Mrs McNab's stern features visibly softened. Then she caught herself on and shook the moment of weakness away.

"Tell the doctor if he wants to come and collect the boys I've no objection," she said. "It'll be nice to have the house to myself for a change."

"Oh, thank you Mrs McNab." Johnny threw his arms around the housekeeper's knees and hugged her. She waited slightly longer than was absolutely necessary before disentangling him and telling him not to be so silly.

"That's settled then," said Morag, and Peter said he'd see her to the gate.

The pair of them strolled down the path together like old friends with Johnny, still not brave enough to ride without someone holding on, pushing his bike behind them.

"It'll be a relief to get something decent to eat for a change," said Peter, under his breath. "She's got to be the worst cook in the world."

"Rock cakes like real rocks," whispered Johnny, and they all laughed.

"Don't be long," called Mrs McNab, sensing perhaps that the joke was on her. "It's time you were both upstairs. I'll just go light the candles." And she disappeared indoors.

"Nine-thirty," snorted Peter, after she'd gone. "Is nine-thirty a reasonable time to expect me to be in my room? Anyone would think I was a baby."

"You could always sneak out when she's gone to bed," said Morag.

"It would be more than my life was worth. If she caught me I'd get skinned alive."

"Why should she catch you? Once she's upstairs, who's to know? Johnny won't tell, will you Johnny?"

Johnny looked none too pleased at the suggestion but he said nothing, just shook his head.

"What about my feet?" said Peter. "They still hurt like mad. I don't think I could go far on them."

"You don't have to. We can sit and chat behind the stone wall at the end of the garden. Where's the harm? Come on. I dare you."

"Peter. Johnny. Indoors now, if you please." Mrs McNab's head emerged from an upstairs window. "And you, young lady, away off home while it's still light, if you don't want the Bogle to get you."

Peter shrugged his shoulders in resignation and raised a hand in farewell. Then he and Johnny trailed inside, Johnny propping his bicycle against the wall by the back door.

Morag waved cheerily at the housekeeper and cycled off into the gloaming for all the world as if she was going home. As soon as she heard the door slam, however, she checked over her shoulder to see whether Mrs McNab had ducked inside again. Having assured herself that she had, Morag dismounted and crouched down behind the dry stone wall, secure in the knowledge that Peter would be out shortly. She'd never yet met a boy who could resist a dare.

She hadn't long to wait. Upstairs, Mrs McNab supervised the boys' bedtime ritual and then retired to her own apartments and the historical romance she'd picked up in the library the day before.

Peter gave her time to settle down then, pulling his jeans and sweatshirt over his pyjamas, he tiptoed into Johnny's bedroom to swear him to silence.

"You go to sleep," he said. "I won't be long."

"What if the Bogle gets you? Mrs McNab said it might get Morag."

"There's no such thing as the Bogle. It's just something made up to scare children into staying in their beds. But I'm not a child. So it doesn't scare me."

"What about dark of the moon?" Johnny persisted. "What about the spooks?"

"Morag said it's not dark of the moon for another couple of days. Besides, you and I know there's no such thing as spooks."

"Not in Hampstead," said Johnny in a small voice.

"Not anywhere," said Peter, firmly. "Now go to sleep."

"Don't go, Peter," pleaded Johnny. "I don't like this house. I'm afraid on my own."

"Oh don't be such a wimp," said Peter, losing patience. "You've got your candle. What are you worried about? Besides, I'll only be gone a little while. I'll be back before you know it."

Before his younger brother could say anything else, Peter slipped quietly downstairs and let himself out into the night. Morag was waiting behind the wall.

"Is Johnny asleep?"

"Not yet, he's worried about the Bogle. What is the Bogle anyway?" he asked, settling himself down on a patch of dry grass. "Some sort of Scottish version of the bogeyman?"

Morag went quiet, quiet as the night that surrounded them, quiet as the grave.

"What's the matter?"

"I don't think I should tell you." Morag studied her hands, as though they were suddenly of immense interest to her.

"Why not?"

"You'll just make fun of me. The way you did when I told you about the witchwoman."

"I won't," said Peter, his curiosity now well and truly aroused. "I promise."

Morag took a deep breath. "Well..." she began. "The Bogle is a sort of entity. A spirit of pure evil. It lives at crossroads. It's supposed to be a combination of all the bad things that have ever happened there."

"Ah," said Peter, "like the burnings and hangings."

"And suicides," said Morag, warming to her subject. "They used to bury suicides at crossroads too. Suicide was a sin so anyone who did away with themself was believed to be damned for all eternity. They couldn't be buried in hallowed ground in the churchyard. The Bogle is supposed to have possessed their souls too."

"Sounds like a nasty piece of work," Peter was fascinated, in spite of himself.

"None nastier," said Morag, seriously. "A supernatural creature formed out of all that negative energy? The sadness of suicides, the fear and agony of witches, the guilt of murderers, the terror of human sacrifices. You don't get much nastier than that."

"So it IS a Scottish version of the Bogeyman?"

"I suppose. Except that the Bogle doesn't just scare you."

"What then?"

Morag looked up under her hair, the whites of her eyes glowing strangely in the half light. She reached out to grasp Peter's wrist and he felt the blood drain from his face.

"If it catches you and touches you and puts its mark on you..." Morag lowered her voice dramatically, "You are destined to die within the year."

Upstairs, Johnny had tried to go to sleep like

Peter had said, but he couldn't help remembering the horrible grey thing that had pursued him in his dreams of the night before. And the night before that. Every night since they'd been in this horrible house. No matter how hard he tried, he couldn't get it out of his head. Every time he started to drop off the smothering fog with its choking smell would invade his mind, shocking him awake again.

He tucked Fred inside his pyjama top to keep him safe. The candle on the bedside table began to gutter, throwing huge, scary shadows on the walls. Johnny curled himself into a ball, putting his hands over his eyes, praying for his older brother to come back and protect him from the grey monster and whatever other nameless horrors were hiding in cupboards and behind doors, just waiting to sneak under the covers as soon as the candle went out.

He must have dozed, for suddenly the grey thing was there, hanging above him, enveloping the bed. The smell nearly suffocated him. He couldn't breathe. Before his terrified gaze a tendril snaked out from the middle of the denseness and reached towards him, groping blindly for his forehead. He shrank back, certain that if it touched him he would never wake up again. He willed himself to come out of the dream, knowing that it was the only way he could save himself. He began to kick his legs, trying to run away, making little mewling sounds in his half-sleep, like a newborn kitten that has lost its mother.

Slowly, the tendril came closer.

In a last superhuman effort, Johnny opened his mouth and screamed with all the lungpower he could muster.

In the room above, Mrs McNab dropped her book and, grabbing her dressing-gown, rushed headlong down the stairs.

She found Johnny thrashing around among his disordered bedclothes, howling with terror. As she came in, he knocked the candle over with one hysterical swipe. The grease ran on to the open book on his bedside table. A yellow flame licked the side of the page, threatening to ignite. Mrs McNab grabbed the water jug and threw the contents over it before it could catch hold. Then she grabbed Johnny and shook him roughly.

"What on God's earth ails you, bairn?" she said. "I thought at the very least the Bogle had got you."

Johnny looked up wildly into the face staring down at him. A cross face. A furious face. A face totally unlike his mother's.

"Leave me alone," he sobbed. "I don't like you. You're scaring me. I want Mummy. I want Peter."

Peter, who at the first scream had leapt to his feet, was at that very moment hobbling towards the house with his heart pounding.

After that, everything seemed to happen at once.

The front door slammed open and Johnny shot through it, hotly pursued by Mrs McNab, black dressing-gown flying, uncombed hair starting from her head like wire wool.

"Peter, Peter," screamed Johnny. "Don't let the Bogle get me."

He slammed into his big brother, almost knocking him over. Peter scooped him up, hugging him tight, calming him down.

"Whoa, whoa," he said. "Relax. Where's the fire?"

"Well might you ask," snarled Mrs McNab. "He's almost set the house alight."

"Don't let the Bogle get me," Johnny snivelled into Peter's shoulder. He was shaking like a leaf.

"Nothing's going to get you," said Peter. "You're safe. I'm here."

"But you shouldn't be here, should you?" said Mrs McNab, nastily. "You should be upstairs in your bed. Instead of out here, in the dark, with this ... this ... hussy."

Peter's patience snapped.

"What have you been saying to him?" he demanded, furiously. "If you've been frightening him I'll tell my dad."

"Me, frightening him? That's rich," snorted Mrs McNab. "He was having nightmares again. You were supposed to be looking after him. You were supposed to be next door. The poor child knocked over his candle he was so terrified. If I hadn't got down promptly we could both have been burned alive in our beds. What is your father going to say about THAT, I'd like to know?"

9

Peter was beginning to wonder if he'd ever get out of the doghouse. This time he'd been grounded. For a whole week. He was to be allowed out of the house but not out of the garden. He was forbidden to communicate with Morag until further notice. And Sunday lunch was cancelled.

"It'll give you the chance to spend some time with Johnny." Mrs McNab had said, severely. "Maybe if you paid him a bit more attention he wouldn't have so many nightmares."

The doctor had come over to plead their case but Mrs McNab was adamant. Rules were rules, she told him, and if he had a few more rules in his own house, it might be better for all concerned.

That had been this morning, and Peter, since he had nothing better to do, had used the day to continue the bike-riding lessons. It had taken all morning and most of the afternoon but by tea-time Johnny was confident enough to wobble up and down the garden path on his own. The small victory pleased him mightily.

"Wait'll I show Dad," he crowed.

"Don't hold your breath," Peter had told him.

At least the engineer had turned up to repair the generator at last. No more candles. No more chance of Johnny setting the house on fire. Johnny was OK, Peter conceded, but he was no substitute for someone his own age. Like Morag. He sighed and resigned himself to seven days of babysitting and boredom.

Morag, of course, had other ideas – as he was to discover later that evening.

He'd been in his room for half an hour but hadn't bothered to change out of his day clothes yet. It was still light and he wasn't even remotely sleepy. He'd tried reading but he couldn't concentrate. Something about the smell of the summer night filtering in through the open window made him restless.

Johnny was in bed already, showered and pyjamaed and, for all Peter knew, fast asleep. Mrs McNab had retired to her rooms. The big old house was quiet and still.

Which is why, when the pebble smashed against the window pane, he almost jumped out of his skin.

He sat up, swinging his legs over the side of the bed, and moving over to the window looked down into the garden.

Morag was standing by the greenhouse in her shorts and singlet, her red hair pulled back in a ponytail for a change. She was just about to hurl another pebble when Peter stuck his head out the window and put a finger to his lips. She mimed was it safe to come closer, and he nodded, so she scurried swiftly across the overgrown lawn at a crouch, ending up directly beneath him.

"Coming out?" she said, *sotto voce*.

Peter shook his head.

"I'm grounded," he whispered. "Didn't your dad tell you?"

"If he did I wasn't listening. Anyway, I'M not grounded. Hang on. I'm coming in."

Before Peter could stop her, she'd shinned up the drainpipe like a monkey and climbed inside.

Peter crossed to the door, looking up and down the dim corridor to make sure no one was in sight. Then he closed it behind him, turning the old-fashioned key in the lock just to be on the safe side.

"I'm not supposed to see you for a week," he said. "If anyone catches us there'll be murders done."

"You worry too much. Who's going to catch us?"

"That's what you said when I sneaked out last night. If I hadn't listened to you then I wouldn't be grounded now."

Somewhere in the house a stair creaked. Peter jumped, looking towards the door, expecting to see the handle turn and Mrs McNab burst in. With what? A kitchen knife? A hatchet?

Morag curled her lip in scorn.

"Relax," she said. "Old houses always make noises in the night."

"Yeah, but not all of them have a mad housekeeper living in the attic."

"I'll just go then, shall I?"

She made to climb out again but Peter stopped her.

"OK, OK," he said. "You're here now. I don't suppose a few minutes is going to matter one way or the other."

Morag plonked herself on the bed.

"That's more like it," she said. "I can't stay long anyway. I only popped over to see how you were coping with solitary confinement."

"I'm bored rigid if you want to know. I thought I might get a chance to sneak down into the basement and have a look around. But Madam keeps all the keys on a ring attached to her belt."

"Where are they now?"

"They used to hang on a hook in the kitchen but since she caught us in the library, she's taken to taking them upstairs with her at night."

"Suspicious."

"Very."

Another board creaked. Peter jumped again as if he'd been stung. Morag grinned at him.

"The state your nerves are in you probably wouldn't have the guts to go down there even if she gave you the key herself."

Peter went red to the roots of his hair.

"That's rich," he said, "coming from someone who believes in the Bogle."

He pulled his face into a grimace and lurched towards her with outstretched arms. "Stay where you are," he said in a hollow voice. "I've come to put my mark on you."

"Don't tempt providence," said Morag. "It isn't funny."

"Oh come on. You don't actually believe that balderdash, do you?"

"All I know is that a lot of people have mysteriously disappeared around Crossmaglen crossroads over the years. And always at dark of the moon."

Peter flung himself down on the bed beside her, propping himself up on his elbows.

"And what's it supposed to look like, this extra from a horror movie?"

"Nobody's ever lived to tell the tale," said Morag. "But they say it's like a vaporous cloud, or a pillar of smoke. Grey, choking. It surrounds you and gets inside you and—"

"I know – and puts its mark on you," snorted Peter. "This I'll have to see."

"You wouldn't laugh if you DID see it. Anyway, you're hardly likely to."

"I didn't think so, somehow."

"That's not what I meant. You're not likely to see it because it only comes out at midnight on dark of the moon and you won't find me or anybody else next nor near the Crossmaglen crossroads then."

"Good grief, you DO believe it."

"Let's just say I'm taking no chances."

"And you have the nerve to talk to me about guts. Admit it. You're scared. You're scared of the Bogle."

"I'm not scared. I'm just being sensible."

"Sensible?" crowed Peter. "You're the least sensible person I ever met. What if I dared you?"

"Why would you do that?."

"You dared me to come out last night. And I did – much good it did me. Well, now it's my turn. Now I'm daring you."

"There's a difference between sneaking out after hours and raising the Bogle," said Morag, heatedly.

"Shhhh. Keep your voice down. OK then, if you're not scared, prove it. When's the next dark of the moon?"

"Tomorrow."

"Perfect. Then I suggest we take our bikes and ride up to Crossmaglen at midnight. That way we can prove once and for all that there's no such thing as the Bogle."

"I thought you were grounded? What if you get caught?"

"By whom? According to you everyone within a hundred mile radius will be tucked up in bed with their teeth chattering."

Morag moved to the window.

"I've got to go," she said.

"So – is it a date, or are you backing out?"

"I'll think about it."

"You're backing out," said Peter, and then... "I DOUBLE dare you."

Morag halted halfway through the window. Enough was enough.

"All right," she said. "It's a date. I'll see you at the top of the road at eleven-thirty."

She slid down the drainpipe, her disembodied voice rising out of the darkness to have the last word. "Just don't say I didn't warn you," she said.

Peter closed the window and flung himself down on the bed, well pleased with having won the game. Tucking his hands behind his head he stared up at the gargoyle faces carved in the wooden ceiling.

"The Bogle," he snorted. "What next? The Abominable Snowman?"

Next door, Johnny turned and twisted in his sleep. He was dreaming again. The same bad dream. He was running, running, and the wraith-like thing was after him – gliding silently, hovering above the trees. Closer and closer it came – like a pestilence, like the spectre of his own death.

Then suddenly he couldn't run any more. His feet were stuck in the mud. He was sinking.

The thing was almost upon him, swooping down on him at the speed of light.

And there was no escape.

10

The next day passed in a mixture of apprehension and impatience. Peter thought it would never end.

He wasn't allowed out of the grounds. So he had to content himself with polishing his bike, playing with his brother and indulging in what his mother used to call "wishing his life away". If he never saw another piece of lego, it would be too soon.

But eventually, evening arrived.

Supper, a particulary unappetizing cold collation of greasy mutton and vinegared beetroot, had been dutifully chewed through and the remains cleared away. Mrs McNab had retired to her rooms and her novel and Johnny was safely tucked up in bed.

Peter waited until the house was completely dark and silent. Or at least as dark as it was going to get this June dark of the moon. Then he waited another half hour to be on the safe side. Finally, when he couldn't stand the suspense a minute longer, he tiptoed down the stairs, past the quietly ticking grandfather clock in the front hall, and eased himself out into the summer night. He'd left the garage door open earlier in the day so that the squeaky hinges wouldn't give the game away. He sneaked inside now and, hefting his bicycle across his shoulders, padded across the gravel to the garden gate. Not until he was safely outside the perimeter wall did he swing himself into the saddle and pedal off furiously in the direction of Crossmaglen.

As he reached the the first bend in the road he checked his watch. It was eleven-fifteen precisely. He glanced over his shoulder at the house, scanning the front for any signs of life.

Nothing stirred.

He grinned, delighted with himself. He'd done it. He'd beaten the curfew. When he got back, at whatever time, no one would even know he'd been out.

But one person knew already.

Johnny.

Cowering under the bedclothes, afraid to go to sleep because of the nightmares, he'd heard his big brother leave his room. At first he thought that Peter had gone to the bathroom. He lay there, shivering, listening for him coming back. But when, after five minutes, he HADN'T come back, Johnny went to investigate. Finding a bolster masquerading as a body under the bedclothes, he realized that something was up.

Scurrying to the window, his heart in his mouth, he was just in time to see Peter moving across the gravel with his bike slung across his back.

Panic seized the little boy. As far as he could see he had three choices. He could stay alone in the dark. He could follow Peter to who knows where. Or he could raise the alarm and get them all into trouble.

He took an instant and painful decision. Clad only in his pyjamas, slipperless and with pulse racing, he fled down the stairs as though the hounds of hell were after him and, grabbing his bike from where he'd left it by the garden gate, wobbled off after his brother.

The first thing that Peter noticed was how quiet it was. Unnaturally quiet. Normally, even at this hour, there should have been SOME sound. The croaking of an occasional frog. Rustling in the bracken by the side of the path as a rat or a vole went about its business. But there was nothing. It was almost as if the night had been trapped in a noise-free zone.

To keep himself company, he began to whistle under his breath. The thin sound sliced into the silence like a radio signal and he stopped again, suddenly certain that, by broadcasting his presence to the surrounding countryside, he was simply setting himself up as a target.

But for what?

"The dreaded Bogle," he thought to himself, and tried to smile at the absurdity of such a thing.

But somehow the smile wouldn't come and Peter found himself wishing that he'd kept his big mouth shut. Showing off in the safety of your own room in the middle of the afternoon was one thing. Being out here, in the wilds, in the middle of the night was something else again.

In the Highlands, as in space, nobody could hear you scream.

A sound behind him made him pull up short, the hairs on the back of his neck bristling.

Somebody – or someTHING – was following him.

"Who's there?" he shouted, listening for an answering call, straining his ears in the darkness.

But there was no reply.

Peter shook himself to get rid of the crawling sensation on his skin and rode off again, telling himself not to be so stupid and childish. But the feeling of a nameless presence tailing him persisted and he found himself riding a little faster, hurrying to his rendezvous with Morag where originally he had intended to be a little late, to make HER wait, to allow her to feel apprehensive, so that she would be extra glad to see him when he did turn up. He had thought this would give him an advantage. He would be the cool, calm knight in shining armour come to rescue the dithering, superstitious damsel in distress.

He slowed down again.

"Get a grip," he muttered. "This is the twenty-first century. Men have stood on the moon. There's no such thing as the Bogle. There's nobody following you. You're just imagining things."

But of course he wasn't.

Behind him, little Johnny, terrified out of his wits at being out in the dark, but even more terrified of being sent back on his own to the house of horrors, crouched behind the boulder where he'd ducked when his brother had called out.

He waited, holding his breath. If he gave himself away now it was back to Mrs McNab and the nightmares. Time enough to let Peter know he was there when they got to where they were going. Wherever that was. By that time it would be too late to send him home.

Not until he heard his brother ride off again did Johnny come out of hiding and pedal off in hot pursuit.

The second thing Peter noticed was the quality of the light. It wasn't the usual mellow blue of most Highland summer nights. It was greenish, almost phosphorescent. Moving through it was like walking along the bottom of a particularly muddy pond. The air was heavy too, and as foul as stagnant water. He felt he had to pedal harder to push his way through it.

The visibility was such he almost rode past Morag before he saw her, hunched over her bike by the side of the road. Her freckled face had never seemed so welcome. But she didn't look her usual cheerful self. Her features were pinched with worry and, although she would never have admitted it, a hint of fear.

"I thought you weren't coming," she said, as if she wished he hadn't bothered. "I was just about to go home."

"I had to wait until the coast was clear," said Peter, and he grinned reassuringly. The last thing he wanted was for her to know he'd been spooked.

"So. Still up for it?" she asked, uncertainly. "Last chance to change your mind."

"Only if you want to change yours?" he said, crossing his fingers behind his back, hoping she'd cry off at the last minute. That way he could save face.

But Morag was made of sterner stuff. She stood up, albeit reluctantly, and climbed on to her bike.

"We'd better get a move on then," she said. "Otherwise we'll be too late."

They rode silently, side by side, through the murky night, as the path rose at first in a gentle gradient and then more steeply towards the crossroads and the standing stone that flanked the triangle of grass at its centre. By the time they reached their destination they were both breathing heavily and slicked with sweat. They parked their machines against the great granite boulder and sat down with their backs to it.

Morag scrunched herself up into a ball, hugging her legs to her chest, resting her chin on her knees. Nobody said a word. The unnatural quiet of the night closed in on them. Claustrophobic. Charged with menace.

"What happens now?" Peter wanted to know.

"Your guess is as good as mine. We wait, I suppose."

"How long?"

Morag squinted at her watch in the half-light.

"As long as it takes. I make it five minutes to midnight," she said, "so we've still got time to run for it."

"I think I can last for five minutes," said Peter.

Morag put her hands over her ears, as though the silence was deafening her. "I'd say it was your funeral," she said. "But unfortunately it's mine too. I don't know why I let you talk me into this."

"Five minutes," said Peter. "Then we'll go. We'll laugh about this in the morning, you'll see."

But the five minutes felt like half an hour. A year. A lifetime. And with each second, the tension grew. It felt like a living thing, buzzing in the blood, sharpening their senses to fever pitch.

At two minutes to, Morag, unable to stand the strain a moment longer, leapt to her feet and taking a flask from her saddle-bag handed it over for Peter to take a swig. "It's lemonade," she said, shakily. "Home-made."

"Hardly the time or the place for a picnic," said Peter, trying to lighten the mood.

"Don't joke," said Morag, furiously. "And be ready to move as soon as it shows."

"Get real," scoffed Peter. "Nothing's going to show."

Now that he was with Morag his bravado of the previous afternoon was beginning to return. That, and the hormones being pumped into his bloodstream by the heightened sense of danger. In some perverse way he was actually beginning to enjoy himself. He checked the time.

"One minute," he said. "I should have laid bets. I could have cleaned up."

"It's not over till it's over," said Morag. "Don't count your chickens."

"Well honestly," said Peter, ticking off the seconds, "you didn't really think anything was going to happen, did you? Fifty, forty-nine, forty-eight..."

He'd got as far as thirty when the cold came down. A sudden freezing cold that descended like a curtain, clutching with a clammy hand.

Morag's teeth began to chatter.

She made a sudden dive for Peter, wrapping her arms round his waist in a vice-like grip. She was shaking like a jelly. He put a protective arm round her shoulders, found he was shaking too.

Then two things happened at the same time. Somewhere down in the valley a church clock chimed midnight. And something thick and viscous rose up out of the centre of the triangle of grass and hung like a malevolent mist, not ten metres away from where they crouched.

A cylindrical column of pulsing matter, dirty grey in colour, it sent out waves of chilling air that froze the two friends to the spot. It had no features as such, but glimpses of toothless mouths and staring eyes momentarily appeared from the dense core only to be swallowed up again in the murk.

Lost souls held prisoner.

Around the outer edges, fronds of vapour curled and uncurled continuously, as though the thing, whatever it was, couldn't wait to grasp the nearest available throat and throttle the life out of it.

But it was the atmosphere that leached out of the apparition that was most horrific. Evil incarnate, heightened by an almost overwhelming stench of putrefaction and decay.

The foul entity hung there, an evil genie escaped from a bottle, silently waiting, biding its time. Then it began to surge forward, flowing towards its intended victims like a tidal wave. When it was almost upon them, a groping tentacle emerged from its epicentre and darted swiftly towards Peter's perspiring forehead.

11

At this point Johnny wobbled over the hill. He was still unsteady on his new bike and, what with the uneven road surface, he had fallen off at least a dozen times on the way. He had skinned his knees and twisted his ankle. But all that was as nothing compared with what faced him now.

He pulled up short, dropping his feet to the ground to steady himself.

There, not three hundred metres away, was the thing he'd been dreaming about for the past two, long, horrible nights.

His nightmare had come to life.

It hovered over Peter and Morag like a malevolent cloud.

Johnny tried to cry out, to divert the monster's attention so they might get away. But the words wouldn't come. Then fear got the better of him. He struggled to turn his bike around, telling himself he would go and get help. In his panic, he caught his foot on a root, overbalanced and fell into the bracken-covered ditch. He lay there, all the breath knocked out of him. He was hidden, safe for the moment at least. Gingerly, he pulled the bike in on top of him and shrank down further, trying to make himself totally invisible.

The grey phantom hesitated, sensing something. The long tentacle retracted, stopping just short of Peter's forehead.

Morag made a strangled sound, something midway between a gurgle and a shriek. It was enough to break the spell. She and Peter let go of each other and, scrambling on to their individual bikes, began to ride furiously away from the crossroads. They shot hell for leather over the rutted track, tyres bouncing off the loose stones, machines veering wildly from side to side. Now Peter knew what Morag had believed all along. The Bogle was more than a fairy story. The Bogle WAS. And it was horrific.

The Bogle let them go, savouring the sport. It chuckled deep inside itself, a vile rasping sound like fingernails tearing at a blackboard. Let them run. Prolong the agony. Allow them to think they were going to get away.

Delusions.

Once the Bogle had flushed out a victim, there was no escape.

So there was no hurry either. A bit of cat-and-mouse only added to the fun.

The creature surged softly after the two desperately fleeing humans, flattening the heather with the wind of its passing. The plan, hatched in the nerve centre that was its primitive brain, was to ALMOST catch them up. Get close enough to breathe its foul breath on the back of their necks. Then to fall back. Let them believe they were getting away. Fill them with false hope. Make the inevitable all the more bitter a pill to swallow.

Such a delicious game. Even though the final result was a foregone conclusion.

Peter and Morag pedalled on desperately, breath exploding in their lungs, legs pumping, hearts racing. Now and again one of them would cast a terrified glance over a shoulder to see whether the frightful thing was gaining. Sometimes it was, sometimes it wasn't. The suspense was unbearable.

They flashed past the point where Johnny lay hidden in the undergrowth. Peter noticed a movement out of the corner of his eye.

"There's something in the ditch," he yelled. "An animal or something."

"Keep going," Morag shouted back. "It might distract that thing."

As if it had heard her, the Bogle slowed to a halt, hovering, sniffing the air. It undulated like a great jellyfish, rotating in a circle. Then it spotted something. A child. Climbing out of the ditch up ahead.

It was much smaller than the other two. But a tasty morsel nonetheless. This was too much to hope for. Many moonless nights had passed since a wandering victim had been foolish enough to stray into the Bogle's territory. Now, in one fell swoop, it looked as though it would be three times lucky.

The creature stilled, resting, charging its batteries while the little one remounted and fled off after the others. It was almost gibbering with fright. The Bogle could feel the vibrations of terror streaking out behind it. An insignificant creature maybe. But capable of strong emotion. A delicious bite to whet the appetite before the main course.

The Bogle spun itself into a fiendish tornado of glee. Then with a low whine, it whirled off in pursuit.

Johnny tried to cry out to the others to wait. But he hadn't enough breath for it. He could hear the soft keening whoosh of the Bogle coming closer. The stench of its foulness made him retch. He began to whimper to himself, trying to wake himself up as he had on the previous evenings.

But this was no dream.

This was desperately, horrifyingly real.

And then suddenly, his front wheel hit a particularly deep rut and he catapulted headfirst into the road.

Just before his head thudded into the rock that

knocked him senseless, he had a brief, vivid image of his mother's face smiling up at him.

Then all was darkness.

The Bogle pulled up beside the small, crumpled form. Nudging it over, it stared down into the unconscious face. Then it drew back in surprise.

The little one was smiling.

This was no good. It prodded the boy, trying to wake him, to generate a bit of horror into those bland features. Such a small, innocent face. The Bogle preferred less insipid victims. Personalities brutalized by disappointment and despair. Egos marinated in envy and greed. This creature hadn't lived long enough to have stored away many sins. Not much guilt here. Hardly any wickedness. Fear though. Insecurity too. And a deep well of sadness at its heart centre. Loss. Abandonment. Despair.

That would have to do.

Waste not want not.

The Bogle coiled down and, with a sigh of pure pleasure, insinuated a tentacle into the flesh between the child's closed lids, connecting at the third eye point, enjoying the flow of feelings. Gradually it absorbed all of Johnny's childhood terrors. His grieving for his dead mother. His anxieties about the future. His sense of helplessness. His confusion because his brother didn't like him and his father was never there. All this turmoil was funnelled up into the well of negative energy. And as it fed, so the Bogle grew, wider and denser and fouler, the energy converting into pure, unadulterated evil.

Eventually, its appetite sated, the appartition withdrew the tentacle back into itself.

Enough.

The child was drained. For now. Humans had a wonderful capacity for survival. As long as it didn't get greedy and take too much at once, the Bogle knew that Johnny's life force would renew itself.

That would be the time to come back for second helpings.

Well pleased with its efforts, energized by the snack, it swung round to follow the others. They were almost over the hill and, although it was certain they wouldn't get far, still it felt a spurt of speed was in order.

It surged over the rocky terrain like an express train. The wind whistled through and around it in a high screeching wail. Up ahead it could sense the fear spurting like a bursting boil from its victim's hunched shoulders. The delectable sensation excited it to increase its pace.

It was almost upon them when, without warning, a woman stepped out into its path.

Arms spread wide, face upturned to the area of dark sky where the moon should have been, she glowed as though she had been painted with starlight. Sparks of power streamed from the ends of her fingers.

The Bogle screeched to a halt.

What was this?

A suicide?

Willing victims didn't usually cast themselves into its path. This was a night to remember and no mistake. The body count had just risen to four.

The ghoul hung motionless, getting the measure of this foolhardy female. Then it suddenly swept forward, its fronds plucking at the long, black hair.

The woman stepped back, spoke without words, sending her thoughts directly into the Bogle's consciousness.

"Dinna come any nearer," she said. "Ye canna harm me. I have the power."

She held one hand up in a staying gesture. Tattooed in the centre of the palm an all seeing eye, bordered with a pentacle, halted the Bogle in its tracks.

The monster growled, deep in its centre. Pointed teeth rose, gnashing from its depths, sank back again into the swirling mist.

"You dinna frighten me," said the woman. "I know your kind. And my mother knew you. And my mother's mother before her."

Visions of flames leapt into the Bogle's mind. A woman tied to a stake, writhing and screaming. It ran a lascivious tongue over its teeth, tasting the agony, sweet even in memory.

"I see you recall my ancestor," said the woman. "Even in her death throes she managed to pass on her power. Her children and her children's children have been holding it against just such an evil day as this. As she was, so am I. So save your strength Bogle. Ye canna harm me. You have taken the wain. But you shall nae have the others now."

"I have a feeling we're going to make it." Morag, up ahead, made to look over her shoulder.

"Don't look. Just pedal," Peter yelled at her. "We're nearly there. I can see the house up ahead."

The Bogle, unaware, focused on the woman. It spoke not a word, but its unholy thoughts transferred themselves into her centre of understanding.

"I shall have all of you," it said. "You first."

It moved forward, a dense rope of sulphurous fog closing round the woman's slender throat, squeezing the air pipe shut. Then it raised her off the ground.

"Look. Look at me," it said, words unspoken. "Look into my depths and know that I am the last thing you will see on this earth. My form, the final memory you will ever hold. And that until eternity."

The woman held her look steady, grey eyes never flinching even though her feet swung clear of the ground, even though she could feel her breath begin to fail. Visions of the pits of hell rose in her mind's eye, like the flames that had devoured her great-great-great-grandmother while the city fathers, those fools that had mistaken her gift of healing for devil worship, had looked on in sanctimonious satisfaction. Still the woman's eyes did not waver, even though she felt herself go giddy from lack of oxygen. Not until the Bogle leaned in to place the mark of death on her did she move, swinging her right arm up to cover her face with the huge silver crucifix.

The Bogle howled like a wounded beast and dropped her to the ground.

Peter and Morag, almost at the house, looked at each other wordlessly and put on an extra burst of speed as the nerve-chilling sound cut the air.

The woman stood up, dusted herself off and placed her hands on her hips.

"You have missed your chance," she said, looking up at her adversary in triumph. "The dawn is coming. And the others are home."

The Bogle rose in a violent swirl to the top of the hill. Too late it realized how it had been tricked. It screeched in fury, leaching its hatred into the pre-dawn sky as the two distant figures turned into the sanctuary of the walled garden.

Then, with a hiss like escaping steam, it sank back down towards the woman.

It would have her at least.

Above the dark ridges of the mountains the grey-green light gradually began softening into gold.

The woman smiled, the first rays of the rising sun gilding her raven-black hair with streaks of mica and mercury. Too late.

The Bogle screeched again, in disappointment this time, baying its frustration out into the hills.

Down in the valley Peter and Morag shuddered and looked at each other in dumb relief. Not until the last echoes of that unearthly cry had died away did Peter at last find his voice.

"You OK?" he said.

Morag took a moment to answer, as though she wasn't altogether sure.

"I think so," she said, eventually.

"I'm sorry," said Peter. "I should have believed you."

"I'm sorry too. I should have had more sense than to take you there."

She turned her bike out of the gate.

"I'd better get home," she said, shakily. "My father will be expecting his breakfast before he goes to work. If I'm not there, he'll worry."

"Will you be all right? Do you want me to come with you?"

"I'll be fine. It's getting light. Dark of the moon is over, for this month at least. You'd better get in before Mrs McNab wakes up."

Peter put a restraining hand on the handlebars, holding her back.

"You won't say anything, will you?"

"Don't be daft. Who would I tell? Who would believe me?"

She rode off slowly, raising a limp hand in farewell.

"See you," she said.

"See you."

Peter had the good manners to wait until she was out of sight. Then, too exhausted to put his bike away, he abandoned it on the path, tottered up the stairs and fell straight into bed.

12

Nobody even noticed that Johnny was missing until the witchwoman brought him home. She arrived in her antiquated van shortly after Mrs McNab had come down to put the kettle on for breakfast. She carried the little boy into the house wrapped in a plaid shawl.

He was still out for the count.

Peter felt he'd only been asleep for five minutes when the housekeeper shook him roughly awake.

"Get dressed and come downstairs," she said, sharply. "Your brother's been found out in the hills in his pyjamas."

Peter pulled on his jeans and followed her groggily down to the library, wiping the sleep from his eyes as he went.

Johnny lay stretched out on the big leather sofa, pale as death.

At the far end of the room, staring out of the window, back-lit by the lately risen sun, stood a tall, dark woman in a long green dress. She turned to face him as he came in. Her clear, grey eyes seemed to look straight through him.

Peter recognized the eyes from the brief glimpse he'd had of her when her hood fell off. And from their reflection in the rear view mirror as he'd sat behind her, the night she had rescued Morag and himself from the haar and brought him home in her van.

Jeannie McClure. The witchwoman.

When Morag had first talked about her, Peter had visualized someone ragged and unkempt. Someone gnarled and bent with a wart on her nose. Someone old and ugly. Jeannie McClure was none of these. She was no more than about thirty, striking rather than pretty, with high cheekbones and black shoulder-length hair. Her red velvet waistcoat was decorated with tiny mirrors which flashed whenever she moved. She wore flat leather sandals and big dangly earrings. More than anything she reminded him of the hippies who sold jewellery down Camden market.

Not like a witch at all.

The most notable thing about her was her stillness. She had an air of quiet serenity, as though she was entirely comfortable with herself and the world. The total opposite of Mrs McNab, who was positively seething with agitation.

Peter nodded "hello", moved over to the couch and looked down at Johnny's small, pale face.

"I don't understand," he said. "What's wrong with him?"

"He's had a fall," said Mrs McNab, as though Peter were somehow to blame. "It's knocked him senseless. I can't imagine what your father's going to say."

"What was he doing out in the hills anyway?" Peter wanted to know.

"Don't play the innocent with me," said Mrs McNab. "He's too young to have thought of this himself. Don't say you didn't put him up to it."

Peter opened his mouth to protest, looked at Mrs McNab's furious face and closed it again. What was the point?

The witchwoman came to the rescue.

"Perhaps he was sleepwalking?" she suggested, observing Peter coolly from across the room.

"Sleepwalking," shrilled Mrs McNab. "Why would he be sleepwalking? What could have possessed him?"

"Maybe he was looking for his mother?" The witchwoman moved towards the unconscious child and stroked back his long blond fringe with a sympathetic hand.

Mrs McNab gasped, drawing her breath sharply into her throat.

Beneath the fall of hair, a livid red mark, about

the size of a fifty-pence piece, stood out angrily against the pale forehead. It looked as though someone had branded the boy with the tip of a red-hot poker.

Peter stared at the mark in horror, suddenly recalling the movement in the ditch, putting two and two together. Johnny must have followed them. And this was the result. The Bogle had got him. What had Morag said? "Once touched by the mark of the Bogle, the victim is doomed to die within the year"? The Bogle had got Johnny and it was all his fault.

He looked up, panic-stricken and found the witchwoman regarding him with her measured, grey stare.

And in that moment he knew for a certainty that she'd seen the whole thing. She knew all about his and Morag's escapades of the night before.

"Where did you find him?" he asked, blushing to the roots of his hair.

"On the path not far from Crossmaglen crossroads," said the witchwoman. "His bicycle was beside him."

"His bicycle?" Mrs McNab sounded slightly hysterical. "I thought you said he was sleepwalking?"

"Sleepriding then," said Jeannie, the slightest hint of a smile playing at the corner of her lips.

The sight of the smile acted on the housekeeper like a red rag to a bull.

"You dare laugh," she shouted. "Bringing the child home at this hour of the morning with the mark of death on him. How do I know you didn't kidnap him in the night? How do I know you didn't entice him out with one of your spells?"

"For what purpose would I do such a thing?"

"It was dark of the moon last night. Respectable people were home in their beds, not roaming the hills. How would I know what devilry you were up to? Maybe you needed him for some unholy experiment? Maybe you wanted to sacrifice him to the Bogle?"

"Mrs McNab," Peter had to raise his voice to make himself heard over the housekeeper's ranting. "Miss McClure brought Johnny home. He could have died out there. You should be thanking her, not accusing her."

Mrs McNab rounded on him.

"And what would you know about it? You who've only just arrived in these parts. Don't let her innocent air fool you. There's more to Jeannie McClure than meets the eye. And you know more about this than you're saying too, young man," she went on. "Nobody's going to tell me that your brother got up in the middle of the night, in the room next door to you, and you didn't hear a thing."

"Shouldn't you be getting him into bed and calling the doctor?" said the witchwoman, mildly. Clearly she was used to this kind of a reaction.

The insults seemed to roll off her like water off a duck's back, rebounding on her accuser, leaving Mrs McNab more frustrated and furious than ever.

"Don't you tell me my duty, Jeannie McClure," she yelled. "This is the bitter end. Here's me out here, all on my own, trying to cope with one boy who refuses to do as he's told," here she shot an accusing glance at Peter, "and one who's so disturbed he goes out in the middle of the night, in his pyjamas, on his bicycle, at dark of the moon. Clearly the child is not right in the head. He needs a psychiatrist, not a housekeeper."

"Maybe he just needs a kind word?" suggested Jeannie.

"Enough," stormed Mrs McNab. "Out. Out of my house. I'm an honest, god-fearing woman. I'll not have the likes of you teaching me my job. Out ... before I set the police on you."

"His bicycle's in the back of my van," said Jeannie, addressing herself to Peter. "Maybe you'd like to come out and get it?"

"That's right. Go and get his bicycle." Mrs McNab lifted Johnny roughly into her arms. He was limp as a wet rag. She narrowed her eyes. "You know more about this than you're saying, Peter Wilson," she said. "Don't think I won't find out about it ... because I will." And she stomped off in the direction of the stairs.

"Sorry about that," said Peter, as he and the

witchwoman made their way outside. "If it was up to me I'd have got rid of her the first day. She's an evil old bat. Unfortunately, it ISN'T up to me."

"No need to apologize," said Jeannie, apparently unconcerned. "I know Fiona McNab of old. She's a poor soul whose husband died young. It was an accident, but she's never forgiven the world for his passing. She's more to be pitied than despised."

"She seems to delight in making my life a misery."

"Don't allow her to. It's the only power she's got. Take that away and she's helpless."

"She certainly seems to have it in for you."

"Her opinion is of no interest to me. Only the ignorant fear what they don't understand. Her hatred can't touch me unless I let it."

She opened the back door of her van, breaking in two the rainbow that had been painted across the bright blue base. Johnny's bike lay among an assortment of wicker baskets and boxes of dried herbs. The front wheel was buckled where it had hit the rut that had caused the boy's downfall. The sight of the damaged machine brought the events of the previous night back to Peter with a jolt.

He lifted the machine carefully and set it on the path to inspect it more closely.

"It's the first time he's ridden it out of the garden," he said.

"The bicycle is the least of your worries," said the witchwoman. "The child has the mark of death on him."

Peter felt the blood draining from his face. A great well opened in his centre. He'd often wished his brother miles away, but he'd never have wished this on him, never in a month of Sundays.

"I didn't mean it," he said. "I didn't even know he was awake."

"Of course you didn't mean it," Jeannie reassured him. "Only a fool or a madman would think that you did."

"Or a Mrs McNab."

"You must try not to lay blame. Especially on yourself," said Jeannie. "Blame never helped anyone. You decided to go. But he decided to follow."

"So you did see it? I didn't imagine the whole thing?"

Jeannie nodded. "Yes, I did. And no, you didn't. But don't expect me to stand up in court and swear to anything."

"If it had to take somebody, why didn't it take me? I'm the one who started it. Why Johnny? What did he ever do to deserve such a thing?"

The witchwoman moved round to the front of the van and climbed into the driving seat. The door was decorated with spirals and stars. At any other time Peter would have said "neat" but now he was too numb to notice.

"Sometimes we're just in the wrong place at the wrong time," she said, enigmatically. "Mrs McNab will be sending for the doctor now, but I fear it will do no good."

"Don't say that," said Peter. "He must be able to do something?"

"Modern medicine's a wonderful thing." Jeannie McClure started the engine. "But some things are beyond its scope. If you need me," she added, "you know where I am."

"No I don't," shouted Peter, as she drove off. "Anyway, what could you do?"

The witchwoman stuck her head out the window.

"You'd be surprised," she said. "Morag knows the way."

Then she bounced off towards the High Hills.

"But I'm not supposed to see Morag," Peter muttered to himself, picking up the mangled bike and trundling it into the garage. "More's the pity." Then he made his way upstairs to see how his brother was faring.

The prognosis was not good.

Johnny lay in his bed, white as a sheet, still as a corpse. Small for his age at the best of times, he looked like he'd shrunk overnight. The mark on his forehead, on the other hand, seemed to have grown bigger in the short time that Peter had been outside. It pulsed faintly in the twilight of the curtained bedroom. Like a feeding leech.

Mrs McNab hovered over him like an ill omen.

"Probably just concussion?" said Peter, hopefully. "Probably just bruised himself when he hit the ground?"

"Probably brain damage," said Mrs McNab, bitterly. "I'm away for the doctor ... and to call your father. Don't you dare move from his side while I'm gone."

"Couldn't we wait until we see what the doctor says before you call Dad?" pleaded Peter. "He hates to be interrupted when he's at work. No use worrying him if it's not serious."

He looked down at the small, wan face.

Not serious. Who was he kidding?

"You were in charge, remember?" he added cunningly. "I wouldn't want you to get into trouble."

Mrs McNab looked at him from under hooded lids. She pursed her lips.

"Well," she said, suddenly changing her tune. "Maybe it would be best to have a professional opinion first. We'll discuss it later. I'll be back in half an hour."

Peter pulled over a chair and sat by the bed, listening while the car started up and pulled out of the drive. Only when sound of the engine had died away in the distance, when he could be sure that no one was around to see, did he lean forward and take Johnny's limp hand in his own. It felt clammy and cold, like a dead fish. He rubbed it gently, trying to coax some warmth into it. But his brother never stirred.

Peter felt a great surge of guilt overwhelm him.

"Oh Johnny," he said, close to tears. "I didn't mean it, really I didn't. I'm so sorry. Please don't die."

13

Dr Sutherland duly arrived with Morag in tow. The week when Peter was forbidden to speak to her wasn't up yet. But everyone had other things on their minds, so the pair of them retreated to the bottom of the garden where he filled her in on what had been happening.

"You remember I said I saw something in the ditch? I thought it was an animal. It must have been Johnny."

"How did he get there?"

"He must have followed us on his bike. You should see the state of it. It's a write-off."

"That's the least of your worries."

"That's what the witchwoman said."

"Do you think she knows?"

"Of course she knows."

"What if she tells?"

"Then we're both in trouble."

"We're in trouble either way," said Morag. "If Johnny comes round, the whole world will know."

"I don't care if the world and his wife knows," said Peter, fiercely. "Just as long as he does come round."

"I thought he was in bed when you left."

"So did I. I should have checked. It never occurred to me."

"Maybe he just hit his head when he fell," said Morag, clutching at straws.

"Not much hope of that," said Peter, gloomily. "He has a mark in the middle of his forehead the size of a blood orange."

Upstairs Dr Sutherland was studying the very mark. It had gone a nasty green colour. He pursed his lips and leant forward to place his palm across it. It was warm to the touch and throbbed gently under his hand.

"Must have hit a rock when he came off the bike," he said.

"Let's hope that's ALL it is," said Mrs McNab.

Johnny was still spark out. But he no longer lay still and peaceful as he had done before. The smile that had so infuriated the Bogle had been wiped from his face to be replaced by a worried frown, and he muttered constantly in his delirium, strings of unconnected words that made no sense.

"He's concussed, obviously," the doctor went on. "Should have been wearing a crash helmet."

"He's only just learned to ride the thing," said Mrs McNab, plaintively. "What was he doing out there, in the middle of the night, in his pyjamas?"

"Who knows what goes on in a child's mind, especially one that's recently lost his mother?"

"Jeannie McClure said he was out looking for her," snorted the housekeeper.

"It's a possibility, I suppose?"

This was not what Mrs McNab had wanted to hear. She wanted the doctor to say that Jeannie McClure was a wicked hussy and ought to be locked up, which is what Mrs McNab would have done with her given half a chance.

Johnny picked nervously at the sheets, fingers and lips never at rest.

"The brain's working anyway," said Dr Sutherland. "Otherwise there'd be no movement, no speech. Head injuries are bothersome things," he observed. "A law unto themselves really."

He sat down beside Johnny and lifted the boy's eyelids one at a time.

"Pupils are the same size so there's no swelling, which means, with any luck, no seepage into the brain."

He placed two fingers under the boy's right ear and checked his watch with the pump of blood against his fingertips.

"Pulse is a little slow," he said, "but that's no bad thing."

Pulling back the covers he ran expert hands over the thin body.

"No bones broken," he said. "Mind you, he could do with a bit of meat on him. You're not starving the child are you, Fiona?"

"Eats like a sparrow," said the housekeeper. "No appetite at all. Poor wee mite."

"Pity. He could do with a bit of extra strength to pull him through."

"Should we be getting him to the hospital, do you think?"

The doctor nodded and stood up.

"Aye, I'll give them a ring, get them to send an ambulance. Best have him where he can get immediate attention if he worsens. The next twenty-four hours are critical."

Mrs McNab looked down at the small, pinched face.

"Poor, motherless bairn," she said. "I'm loath to call his father. He's in Brazil."

"I wish I could say not to worry him at this juncture. The man's got enough on his plate trying to keep hearth and home together. I remember when Moira died..." He shook the thought away. "But you'd best let him know, just to be on the safe side. Although my own opinion is that the boy will probably come out of it of his own accord."

"You realize that last evening was dark of the moon?" said Mrs McNab.

"So?"

"Well ... the mark."

"Fiona McNab. How old are you?"

"That's for me to know and you to find out," said the housekeeper, bristling.

"You forget I was at school with you," said the doctor. "So I know you're old enough to know better."

"But your own wife..."

"My wife's headlights failed and she went over a cliff. That's the beginning and end of it."

"So you don't think?"

"No, I DON'T think, and if you had any gumption, neither would you."

"Then what about that woman bringing him home?" said Mrs McNab, darkly.

"If by 'that woman' you mean Jeannie McClure then all I can say is that she's a gentle soul who makes herbal face creams to sell at craft fairs, who never did anybody a button of harm, and who minds her own business. Which is more than I can say for some people."

"You know the family history," said Mrs McNab, huffily.

"I do. And a sorry tale it is. A succession of poor old wifeys hounded by the great and the good. If it were still allowed you'd probably be the first one lighting the faggots. You, who know first hand how hurtful gossip can be."

"That's not the same thing at all," said Mrs

McNab, bridling. "What they said about me was slander."

"It's exactly the same thing. It's about ruining reputations. The witchwoman indeed. Don't make me laugh."

Down in the garden Peter and Morag were also discussing Jeannie McClure.

"She said she'd be there if I needed her," said Peter. "What do you suppose she meant by that?"

Morag was evasive.

"How should I know?" she said.

"Will you take me to see her? She said you knew the way."

Morag coloured. "I may do," she said.

"So what's the problem?"

"My daddy doesn't approve of me going up there. He says it's a load of superstitious nonsense."

"And what do you think?"

"I'm not telling. You'll only start laughing at me again."

"After last night I'm past laughing at anything."

Morag's eyes took on a strange glitter. "I think she's got power. Old knowledge. It's a gifting. Passed on in the genes from mother to daughter. You can't learn it."

"So you think she might cure Johnny with some mumbo-jumbo magic?" Peter couldn't keep the scorn out of his voice.

"Why do I bother talking to you?" Morag flared.

"You're a – a – a heathen. I wish I'd never taken up with you."

"*I'm* a heathen? That's rich. I wish I'd never taken up with you. Then my brother wouldn't be lying upstairs at death's door."

"Oh, so now it's all MY fault?"

"Well, it's certainly not MINE."

"Is it not? Who didn't even bother to check if the boy was in bed? Who wanted to prove that there wasn't a Bogle? You didn't believe in that either, did you?"

Morag stood up and flounced back to her father's car. Peter let his temper cool before he followed her.

"OK," he said. "Calm down. I'm sorry. There is a Bogle. I didn't believe it until I saw it. But I believe it now."

"And that's supposed to make everything all right?"

"I said I was sorry."

"Apology accepted." But Morag still had an edge of anger in her voice.

"So will you take me to see the witchwoman then? For Johnny's sake? She said your father wouldn't be able to do anything for him."

"On one condition."

"What?"

"That you don't sneer. If you sneer, I'll never speak to you again as long as I live."

"I promise I won't sneer."

"Or laugh."

"Or laugh."

"All right. In that case, I'll take you."

"When?"

"First thing tomorrow morning. I'll meet you at the head of the glen straight after breakfast."

Peter was about to say OK when a sudden unearthly wailing filled the air, like the sound of a soul in torment. Morag flung herself at him, wrapping her arms round his neck. At which point Dr Sutherland emerged from the house with Mrs McNab at his heels. She stared, scandalized at the sight.

Morag withdrew, covered in confusion. Dr Sutherland grinned.

"You're very jumpy all of a sudden," he said to his daughter. "It's only the ambulance coming to collect Johnny."

14

The next day dawned bright and clear. Peter wondered whether he would never get used to the fickleness of the Highland weather. Riding along the path, the smell of heather in his nostrils, the sound of crickets in his ears, he wished he could forget that Johnny was in danger. And that he had put him there.

He wished that dark of the moon had never happened. That he could just relax and enjoy the day.

But when he reached the head of the glen and the huge standing stone loomed up on the horizon, the whole thing came back with a rush. He was suddenly seized with a desire to turn tail and run. He felt somehow as though the Bogle had lured him here, that it hadn't been his and Morag's idea at all.

He could see Morag's small figure sitting with her back against the stone. Maybe if he turned and went back now...

Then his friend stood up and waved and he pulled himself together. Even so he had a hard time conjuring up a smile to greet her with.

"You look like death," she said.

"Nice to see you too," said Peter, propping his bike against the standing stone beside hers and squatting down. "I don't feel so hot."

"How's Johnny?"

"Still with us – just. I'm worried to death about him. So is Dad. He's on his way home."

Morag gave him a quick hug. He hugged her back. It felt good.

"Have you had your breakfast yet?" she said, disengaging herself.

Peter shook his head.

"I skipped out before Mrs McNab surfaced," he said. "Thought it was safest. I'm still officially grounded, remember?"

Morag raised her eyebrows.

"Don't worry," said Peter. "I left a note this time. Said I was going for a spin to clear my head and I'd be back by lunchtime."

"Good thought," said Morag. "The last thing we need is for her to be alerting Interpol."

She rummaged in her bike bag and presented him with a package.

"Carrot cake," she said. "Made it myself."

Peter started to wolf it down. He hadn't realized he was so hungry.

"Hey," he said, "this is fantastic."

"No need to sound so surprised. I've been cooking for Daddy since I was ten and I haven't poisoned him yet."

"Ten. That's early."

"It was self-defence. He's the only person I know who can burn water. We'll leave the bikes here," she went on. "The path to Jeannie's is too steep to ride. How are the feet?"

"Better. I borrowed my Dad's hiking boots and I've two pairs of socks on."

"Good. Then let's go."

Morag hadn't been exaggerating when she said it was a steep climb. The path led them up the glen, past the tree line until they hit an escarpment of shale and loose stones. From there they slid and scrambled up still higher to where nothing grew but scrub-grass and lichens. The air was thinner the higher they went and Peter found himself panting to keep up.

"Not far now," Morag encouraged him, indicating the small white building he'd spotted on the day of their first outing.

Set against the skyline, the cottage clung precariously to the mountainside like a limpet, looking as though, at any moment, it might topple into the valley below.

"How on earth does she get a car up here?"

"There's a back way," said Morag. "It's steep but it's driveable."

"Why didn't we come up that way?" puffed Peter. He was feeling lightheaded and his knees were threatening to go on strike. "We could've brought the bikes."

"Because we'd've had to go right round the whole mountain and up the other side to get there, you barm-pot. It'd've taken us until next Thursday. Stop moaning. We're there."

And indeed they were, stepping as though across an invisible line, straight from the bleak mountainside into a small, cultivated herb garden overrun with rock roses and mountain daisies.

Jeannie came to the door to greet them. She'd abandoned her flowing dress for a pair of jeans and a painter's smock and her black hair was secured on top of her head with a coloured clip.

"Come away in," she said. "I've been expecting you."

The interior of the cottage was painted in bright shades of blue and yellow. It smelt of honeysuckle and heather and wild thyme. There were plant-pots everywhere, lining the window-sills and stacked on the shelves. Great bunches of herbs hung from the ceiling to dry and in one corner a half-woven wicker basket lay beside an old-fashioned rocking chair. The square pine table that dominated the room was covered in glass jars and a stack of handwritten labels which Jeannie had apparently been sticking on just before they arrived.

"There's a craft fair on at Auchterarder this Saturday," she said, by way of explanation. "I was just getting my stock ready." She shifted the bottles to one side. "You'll be wanting some tea."

As she filled a kettle from a small water crock and put it on the calor gas stove to boil, a huge ginger cat emerged from beneath the table and insinuated itself round Peter's legs. He bent down to tickle its ears and it purred with pleasure.

"Take no notice of Ariel," said Jeannie. "He'll be all over you like a bad rash."

"How did you know?" asked Peter.

"Know what?" The witchwoman spooned tea into a big red pot while Morag set out cups and saucers, milk and sugar. She was obviously no stranger to the place.

"You said you were expecting us," said Peter. "How did you know we were coming? Did Morag tell you?"

The witchwoman turned and looked at him, the cool grey eyes holding him in thrall. They seemed to expand until the room and everything in it had disappeared and only the eyes were left.

"You'd be surprised what I know." Jeannie's voice filled his ears like the cat's purr, coming from everywhere and nowhere.

Peter suddenly felt very wobbly. He sat down on the rocker with a thump.

"It's the altitude," said Jeannie, handing him a cup of tea. "Drink this – it'll make you feel better."

Peter wondered whether it was safe to drink anything in that house or if, like Alice in Wonderland, he might suddenly find himself shrinking? He took a sip. It was the best tea he had ever tasted, hot and strong and sweet with just a hint of aniseed. It perked him up straight away.

"I take it this is not a social call," said the witchwoman. "How *is* your brother?"

Peter thought of Johnny, small and pale in his hospital bed. When he'd left him the previous evening in that comfortless, sterile room, he'd felt an overwhelming sense of guilt. It flooded back now, souring the tea.

"He's in hospital," he said. "He's still unconscious as far as I know. They're doing tests."

"They willnae find anything," said Jeannie, matter-of-factly. "What ails Johnny comes from another reality. Their machines willnae be able to detect it."

Peter thought of all that space-age technology negated by something older and darker than time.

"So what's the answer?" he said, desperately. "If they can't help what can we do? You've seen the state he's in."

"I told you. Modern science is a wonderful thing but it has no power against something like the Bogle."

"But you have the power, don't you, Jeannie?"

Morag spoke up. "You'll be able to help, won't you?"

"I'll try." The witchwoman stared into the middle distance and pursed her lips. "But I cannae do anything until next dark of the moon."

"But that's nearly a month away," said Peter. "By that time Johnny could be..." The words stuck in his throat.

The big red-gold cat leapt into Jeannie's lap, shaking her out of her reverie. She shoved him down and stood up, and the animal immediately transferred himself to Morag.

"No," said the witchwoman, reading his thoughts. "He'll no be dead. That's not the Bogle's way. It likes to keep the victim alive for as long as possible. Sipping rather than gorging. It gets more nourishment that way."

"But surely there's SOMETHING we can do?" Peter sounded frantic.

He WAS frantic.

Last evening Dr Sutherland had tried to cheer him up, telling him not to worry, that Johnny was in the best place, that it would all be all right. But it hadn't worked. Peter still felt like a traitor. He didn't think he could stand that feeling for another month.

"We can make preparations," said the witchwoman, laying a calming hand on his arm. "Thorough preparations. We'll need to take it where it lives, do you see? Strike at the heart of the lair."

"Beard it in its den," said Morag, with a shudder.

"Exactly. And we cannae do that until it comes out. And it only comes out at..."

"I know, I know," said Peter. "It only comes out at blasted dark of the moon."

And he had to be content with that. At least for the time being.

15

The following day Mark Wilson arrived back, jet-lagged and frazzled. He'd been given compassionate leave of forty-eight hours. The work he was doing for the company was vital and they couldn't spare him for any longer. If the crisis wasn't resolved by then they told him, they would regretfully have to replace him.

By that time Johnny had been discharged from hospital and was back in his own bed. He'd been given every appropriate test that modern medicine could devise from CAT scans to lumbar punctures but, as Jeannie had predicted, no physical cause for his illness could be found.

When his harassed father arrived at the bedside, Dr Sutherland was forced to confess himself stumped.

"You can see from the scan that there's no brain damage," he said, handing Johnny's father the Xrays. "It would seem he's in some sort of traumatic coma."

"So, how long until he likely comes out of it?" Mark Wilson ran his hands through hair still sticky from the jungle heat. His mouth tasted like the bottom of a birdcage and he hadn't had a shower in two days.

"He's been out of it once," said the doctor. "Just briefly. During the second night in hospital he came round and started screaming about some 'thing' in the corner that was trying to get him. Woke up every patient in the ward. Scared the daylights out of most of the night staff. Then he passed out again."

"He's always been prone to nightmares," said his dad, wearily. "But they've got worse since the accident."

He slumped down on the bed. He hadn't realized how thin Johnny was. The lump that the small body made under the bedclothes was hardly bigger than the lump he felt in his throat. Not Johnny too. Not after...

"Is there anything I can do to bring him round?" he said, pulling himself together.

"Sometimes external stimulation will do it. Music. Does he have a favourite song?"

"Not that I know of."

"Or reading. Does he have a favourite book? "

"I've no idea."

The doctor, who had sung Morag to sleep

128

practically every night when she was little and read *The House at Pooh Corner* till it was so dog-eared he'd had to stick it together with sellotape, tried another tack.

"Aye well, a recognizable voice can pull them back. You could just try talking to him. It might help."

"What about?"

"A favourite hobby. Some trip you've taken together. Things that you like to do at the weekend. Anything that might encourage him to regain consciousness."

Mark Wilson, whose life revolved around his work and who had left all that side of things to his dead wife, found himself at a loss. What was Johnny interested in? Or Peter for that matter? He hadn't a clue. He suddenly realized that his sons were almost strangers to him. He leant over the bed.

"Johnny," he said, gently. "Johnny. It's Dad. Can you hear me?"

Not a flicker.

Mr Wilson took the small limp hand in his own large, capable one. The one with which he had done all the practical things around the house when he'd come home on leave. That was his role. The fixer. The big, strong man. His own father had expected him to be seen and not heard. It was the only role- model he had. He remembered Johnny trying to help once, wanting to hammer in nails when he was mending something. And how brusque he'd been, telling him not to "get in the way". He hadn't meant to hurt him, bitterly regretted it now. Looking down on his son's face, the eyes squeezed tight shut as though trying to block out some unimaginably horrible sight, he felt a great surge of emotion and tried again to get through to him.

"Johnny. It's me. Dad. Open your eyes, there's a good boy."

But there was no response.

He looked up at the doctor, in helpless desperation.

"Is he in pain?" he asked.

"Not as far as I can tell. Not physical pain anyway."

"I don't understand. What other kind is there?"

"Well, you can see by his face that he's obviously in some kind of mental distress."

Mr Wilson stroked Johnny's long fair fringe back from his forehead, then drew his hand back sharply as though he'd been stung.

"Good Godfathers," he said. "What's that?"

The bruise had spread and turned livid. Between the eyes it was almost black. From there it spiralled out, moving through shades of putrid green to a bilious yellow at the edges. Purplish tendrils snaked out to the hairline. The whole thing pulsed faintly in the half light like a malevolent spider waiting to spring.

"At first I thought it was just where his head had

come in contact with the ground when he came off the bike," admitted the doctor. "But a normal bruise would have done its work and started fading by now."

"So what is it then? A virus. Bubonic plague. What?" Mark Wilson was bone tired and his patience was wearing dangerously thin. He was a practical man and he wanted practical answers.

"Well." The doctor paused. "You may not like this ... but I have a feeling it may be psycho-somatic."

Without warning, Johnny suddenly sat bolt upright in bed. His eyes, wide and staring, were fixed on a point somewhere over Mark Wilson's left shoulder. He grabbed his father's arm in a vice-like grip.

"Don't let it get me, Dad," he wailed.

Mark Wilson gathered the small frail body into his arms, hugging the boy to him, protecting him. But from what? He looked over his shoulder, to the darkened corner under the eaves, following his son's terrified gaze. There was nothing there.

"Nothing's going to get you," he said. "Not while I'm around."

Cupping the boy's chin in his hand, tilting the pale face towards him, he looked into the frightened eyes.

"What is it, Johnny? What are you afraid of?"

"The Bogle," said Johnny, desperately. "The Bogle. It's in the corner. Can't you see it?"

"There's nothing there, Johnny," said his dad. "It was just a bad dream."

"It's there," moaned Johnny. "It's there. It's there. It's there."

Then he collapsed back on his pillows, eyes closed, mouth working, fingers plucking at the bedclothes.

Mark Wilson looked at the doctor in bewilderment.

"Help me out here," he said. "The Bogle. What's the Bogle?"

Dr Sutherland put his hands in his pockets, moved to the window, looking out into the dark hills.

"There's a legend in these parts," he said "Not that I'm giving it any credence mind you, but there's this ... this Hobgoblin thing ... called the Bogle."

"Go on."

"It's a kind of amalgamation of all things evil. It feeds on the souls of humans. I know ... I know..." He held up a hand to stop Mr Wilson from interrupting. "It's supposed to live at the crossroads and to come out at midnight on dark of the moon."

"Dark of the what?"

"It's the opposite of full moon, the night between the end of the old moon and the beginning of the new. It was traditionally a time when witches wove their wickedest spells. And midnight is the darkest hour of dark of the moon. So if you happen to be around at that time and the Bogle catches you and –" he paused, to give what he was about to say extra emphasis – "puts his mark on you ... then you are destined to die within the year."

Mark Wilson exploded.

"I don't believe I'm hearing this," he shouted. "You're telling me my son's been cursed by some Scottish bogeyman. You ought to be struck off."

"No, of course I'm not saying that. What I'm saying is that Johnny might believe it."

"Why? What in God's name would make him believe such a thing?"

"Well, the night he was out wandering ... the night Jeannie McClure found him ... the night he had his accident ... was dark of the moon."

"This is ludicrous. Why would Johnny think this Bogle had got him? Where would he have heard about it? He hasn't been here five minutes."

"Someone must have told him. Someone who was trying to frighten him."

"Who would want to frighten Johnny? He's only a child."

"Someone who wanted to keep him in line, perhaps?"

"You're not suggesting Mrs McNab?"

"I'm not suggesting anything," said the doctor. "All I'm saying is, it would do no harm to ask."

But Mrs McNab, when confronted, stoutly denied the suggestion.

"I may have mentioned it in passing, but not to frighten the child. If you're looking for someone to blame you want to try Jeannie McClure. She's the one brought him home. It's well known she has the evil eye."

Mark Wilson rolled *his* eyes heavenwards.

"I'm surrounded by lunatics," he said.

"Or else he's got it from Morag," Mrs McNab steamrollered on. "Peter's been seeing her on the sly even though he wasn't supposed to."

"Who's Morag?"

"My daughter," said the doctor. "She and Peter are of an age. They're good company for each other."

"Company, is it?" snorted Mrs McNab. "Up to all sorts. Out to all hours. Got caught in the haar and I almost had to call out the mountain rescue people. Then Peter sneaked out to see her in the middle of the night when I was in bed and Johnny nearly set the house on fire. And she all over him like a dose of the measles. Shameless, I call it."

Mark Wilson looked to the doctor for confimation or denial. The doctor shrugged his shoulders as if the whole thing were out of his hands.

"You cannae very well gag and bind them," he said. "Youthful high spirits is the truth of it. And Jeannie McClure's a good soul. She'd never knowingly harm a child."

Mark Wilson looked down at his younger son, tossing and turning on his disordered bed.

"Well, clearly somebody's harmed him," he said, grimly. "And there's only one person left as far as I can see."

He turned to the housekeeper, holier than thou in her sensible frock and low-heeled shoes.

"Thank you, Mrs McNab," he said. "You may go. Send Peter down to the library, will you? I'll see the doctor out."

16

As it happens Peter was in the library already, absorbed in the book he'd lent to Morag. She'd lent it to Jeannie and Jeannie had returned it on the morning they'd been to visit her.

As Jeannie had said at the time, it made "interesting reading".

It was all about the witch-hunts in Scotland, and the whole chapter devoted to the McClures of Drumnadrochit was an eye-opener, to say the least.

Apparently the house, this house, had belonged to the McClure family right up to the time when the last witch, the present Jeannie's great-great-great-grandmother, had been burned at the stake on a trumped-up charge of raising the Bogle to do away with some land factor who was on his way to see the Laird on business. They'd found the poor man at the bottom of a cliff with not a single bone in his body intact.

The Laird had had his eye on the house for years but Jeannie wouldn't sell. On the premise that it was "an ill-wind" he used the factor's death to accuse Jeannie of witchcraft and before her ashes were cold, he had confiscated the property and moved himself and his large family in there.

But Jeannie had had the last word. With her dying breath she had cursed the house and all who lived in it. None would die peacefully in it, she had warned, until a McClure once more lived under its roof.

The Laird and his six sons had all perished in the ill-fated 1745 rebellion, following Bonnie Prince Charlie's banner. None of them had quick, clean deaths. Three were tortured by "The Butcher" Cumberland before being hanged. The other three lingered with suppurating battle wounds. One succumbed to gangrene and had his legs cut off before he died of shock. One got blood-poisoning and expired screaming in agony. The last, and youngest, a lad not much older than Peter, couldn't scream, having contracted lockjaw, but his eyes spoke of his excruciating pain, the muscles in such spasms that they broke his back, before he eventually passed away. The Laird himself was hung, drawn and quartered in the village square on the very spot where Jeannie McClure had been burned alive. Although it has to be said that the crowd was considerably smaller and lamentably short of men.

The Laird's wife went mad and threw herself from the roof of the big house.

His two daughters both married Englishmen and moved south which, in the Drumnadrochit of the time, was considered to be a fate WORSE than death. They both died in childbirth.

Peter shuddered. So – the house was cursed.

He had just got to the bit where not a single owner since had died peacefully in their beds, when his dad stormed in, launching his attack almost before he'd closed the door.

"What have you been saying to Johnny?" he said.

"About what?"

"About this Bogle thing."

Peter blanched.

"Ah, I see you know what I'm talking about?"

"Nothing. I didn't say anything. Maybe Mrs McNab..."

"I've already spoken to Mrs McNab, so don't try to blame it on her."

Mr Wilson began to pace up and down. He'd been trying to keep his temper under control but now, fuelled by his genuine concern for Johnny and his utter exhaustion from the long trip, it threatened to get the better of him.

"I don't understand you, Peter," he said, gritting his teeth. "I really don't. I leave you in charge. I trust you to look after your brother while I'm away and the minute my back's turned you're frightening the life out of him with these stories about supernatural monsters putting a death-mark on him."

"But Dad..." Peter tried to get a word in edgeways.

"Don't 'but Dad' me." His father obviously wasn't having any, had made up his mind, didn't want to listen to explanations or excuses. "The doctor says his coma's been brought on by Johnny's fear of this Bogle thing. He must have got the idea from somewhere. I assume that you and your friend Morag thought it was funny, scaring him half to death? Well, this time it's backfired. This time you've gone too far."

Peter said nothing. Clearly his dad had no idea about the Bogle-hunting episode. And, considering his present mood, Peter wasn't about to enlighten him.

"You know how easily upset he is," his dad went on. "You know how impressionable he's been since your mother..."

"Why do you always blame me for everything?" Peter didn't want to discuss his mother. "It's not fair. None of this would have happened if you hadn't moved us up here."

He waved the book under his dad's nose.

"You know this house is cursed, don't you?"

"Cursed?" His dad looked at him as though he'd gone stark, staring mad.

"Yes, cursed," said Peter. "By Jeannie McClure.

The last witch to be burned in Scotland. She cursed the house and everybody who lived in it."

His father snatched the book from him.

"Where did you get this garbage?" he said, grimly.

"It belonged to the last owner, Mr Blane," said Peter. "He went out at dark of the moon and was never seen again."

Mark Wilson flung the book to the other side of the libary. It hit the fireplace with a thud and slid down to settle in the empty grate.

"Will you stop talking nonsense?" he shouted.

But Peter had started now and he COULDN'T stop.

"They say Mrs McNab murdered him because he wouldn't marry her. SHE wanted the house. They say she buried him in the cellar."

Peter's dad put his hands over his ears.

"Stop. Stop. Stop," he yelled.

Peter stopped.

His father sat down on the couch and put his head in his hands.

"Where did you hear such rubbish?" he said.

"It's common knowledge," said Peter. "Why do you think the house has been empty for so long? Why do you think it was so cheap? Morag said the estate agent..."

"Morag eh?" his father cut him off. "The more I hear about this girl the less I like her. No wonder Mrs McNab thinks she's a bad influence."

"She isn't a bad influence," Peter objected. "Mrs McNab's the one. She makes us go to bed at 9.30. We're not allowed to touch Mr Blane's books. She grounds me for nothing. And her cooking stinks."

His father looked up.

"Anything else?"

"You don't have to live with her," said Peter, feebly. "She's like something out of the Dark Ages."

Mark Wilson stood up and faced his son. He was a tall man, all of six foot three, but Peter almost came up to his shoulder. Where had the time gone? It seemed only yesterday that he was in his pushchair. He thought about what the boys had had to put up with over the last six months. The loss. Mary had been the perfect mother, had left a hole that he didn't know how to begin to fill. He felt the anger subside and reached out to place his hands on Peter's shoulders. It felt awkward. He was not a tactile man.

"Look, son," he said. "Mrs McNab is the best I can do at the moment. And you know she couldn't have murdered anyone and buried them in the cellar. If she had, she'd be in jail by now. She's a bit strict, I'll give you that. But she's honest and reliable. Good grief, have you any idea how difficult it is to get a housekeeper out here?"

"Why didn't you leave us in Hampstead then?" said Peter, sullenly. "We could have got a housekeeper there, no trouble."

Mr Wilson dropped his hands and turned away.

"There's no talking to you, is there?" he said. "We've been through all this before. You're here now and you might as well make the best of it. Besides, I'm relying on you to stay close to Johnny until he comes out of this."

Peter thought about Johnny, upstairs, sweating and whimpering. He thought about the Bogle. The mark. The curse. Jeannie. Dark of the moon. But he knew he couldn't say to his dad – "He might not come out of it." Instead he said, "Did the doctor say when he might come round?"

"No, he didn't. Dr Sutherland's a pleasant enough man and I've no doubt he means well. But he's a country bumpkin and, in this case, he's clearly out of his depth. If Johnny doesn't improve I'll have to get an expert up here."

He sat down again and looked at the floor.

"I don't know where the money's going to come from." He said. "You might as well know I'm only hanging on to this job by the skin of my teeth. After all that time I had off when your mother died I promised the company that as soon as I moved you up here there'd be no more absences. I gave them my word they could rely on me to be on the ball. Now with this... The oil business isn't secure any more. There are redundancies and cutbacks going on every day. Engineers are two a penny. If I can't deliver the goods there are ten blokes waiting in line behind me, who can. Any more interruptions and I'll be out on my ear."

He glanced up, his eyes red rimmed and desperate. He looked about at the end of his tether.

Peter didn't know what to say. His dad had always been the strong one. The rock. The provider. Distant but reliable. His mum had been the one who had given him and Johnny day to day discipline and affection. But Mum was gone. And Dad was looking distinctly flaky. And Johnny ... what if Johnny really didn't come round? Ever. What if he just wasted away? Suddenly Peter felt as though his whole world was unravelling at the seams.

His dad stood up.

"I didn't want to worry you with all this," he said. "But you're old enough now to know the facts of life. I've got to get some sleep," he added. "I've only got a forty eight-hour pass. We'll talk about this again in the morning."

He stumbled wearily to the door, then turned.

"And I don't want to hear another word about Bogles or curses or bodies in the cellar. Is that understood?"

Peter nodded, dumbly.

Mark Wilson studied his eldest son with a mixture of worry and despair.

"I've got two words for you, Peter," he said. "And I'd like you to think about them, carefully, before tomorrow. Two words. Grow up."

And he went out, closing the door behind him.

For the first time in his life Peter felt totally, utterly alone.

17

Mrs McNab wasn't present at the interview between Peter and his dad but she made sure that she was listening at the door.

What she heard sent her scuttling back to the kitchen, tight-lipped with righteous indignation, but also with the unsettling knowledge that her position wasn't quite as secure as she'd previously thought. Time, she decided, for a visit to the lawyer in Edinburgh who had managed Mr Blane's affairs. If Mr Wilson went bankrupt, if the house was repossessed, she needed to know where she stood.

No sooner had her present employer reluctantly headed off back to South America, with strict instructions that he be kept informed of any change in Johnny's condition, than she announced she'd be taking a day off, "as is my due" and making a trip to the capital.

"I'll be back by teatime," she told Peter. "Until then, I'm leaving you in charge."

"But what about Johnny?" Peter objected. "What if he gets worse?"

"If Johnny gets worse you'll need to call the doctor. I could do no more myself." She gave Peter a hard look. "Although you and I know that what ails him can't be fixed by any doctors."

Peter went beet-red to the roots of his hair.

"I don't know what you mean," he stammered.

"Aye, well, so you say," said Mrs McNab. "Your daddy brought you a mobile phone, didn't he? And the doctor's number is on the hall table. Use your gumption – if you have any. I'll see you later."

And she'd driven off in a cloud of spray, leaving Peter to cope as best he could.

Her defection was further proof, if he needed any, that, as housekeepers go, she was a complete waste of space. And she obviously had some inkling of what had gone on on the "Night of the Bogle". So all in all it would be better if she was out of the house. But unless he could get something definite on her, it looked like she'd be there for the duration.

Now if she really HAD done away with her previous employer, if there really WAS a body in the cellar...

He used the mobile phone to call Morag.

"Can you come over?" he said.

"When?"

"Right away."

"What, in this weather? I'll get drowned."

Outside it was another "soft" Highland day, the rain falling in horizontal sheets across the heather, the sky lower than a snake's belly.

"Ask your dad to bring you when he comes on his rounds."

"What about Mrs McNab?"

"Mrs McNab's gone to Edinburgh for the day. Now's our chance to have a look in the cellar."

"I'll be right over," said Morag. "Don't start without me."

She rolled up half an hour later, the doctor tooting his horn and dropping her off at the front door.

"Daddy says he'll check on Johnny on the way back. Some farmer's caught his hand in the threshing machine and he's got to see to him first."

Johnny was no better. Although his periods of consciousness were getting longer, the weight was falling off him and his bird-like bones had begun to show through almost translucent skin. When he was awake, he was far from happy, his eyes staring into the middle distance at something that wasn't there. And if he wasn't muttering under his breath, a constant stream of nonsense, he was begging and pleading for whoever was with him to "keep the Bogle away". No amount of assurance that there was nothing there could calm him down. Occasionally he would burst into tears, complaining of pains in his chest, more often he would just whimper, like a sick puppy.

As Mrs McNab had said, in one of her less ascerbic moments, it "made the heart bleed to see the state of him."

His father had been almost beside himself when he'd left. But the company was adamant that he couldn't have any more time off. And Mrs McNab, knowing the financial situation, had persuaded him that the best thing to do was get back to work.

"You cannae do him any good, hanging about worrying," she said, matter-of-factly. "The state he's in, he hardly even knows you're here. He'll come out of it when he comes out of it. And as soon as he comes out of it, I'll let you know."

And Mark Wilson had to be content with that.

After he'd left, the doctor continued to call, but there wasn't much he could do. He had told them to get as much liquid into the child as possible but Johnny didn't seem to be able to keep anything down. All in all, he was a sorry sight.

And through it all, the mark in the centre of his forehead continued to spread like a gangrenous wound.

Even when he was dozing, which he was now, Johnny wasn't at peace, his fingers continually picking at the bedclothes, his lips constantly working in his sleep.

"What's he saying?" said Morag, as Peter made a final check before they headed down to the cellar.

"Nothing that makes any sense," said Peter.

"He looks awful thin."

"I know. And that's just in a week. I don't know how he's going to make it until next dark of the moon.

"Jeannie said the Bogle wouldnae kill him. It likes to keep its victims alive for as long as possible."

"I hope she knows what she's talking about."

"Will he be all right while we look in the cellar?"

"Should be. He's only just dozed off. Normally he sleeps for hours at a stretch. Anyway we'll need to chance it. That woman isn't doing him any good. What he needs is a kind face when he comes round, not somebody who looks like Dracula's mother."

Morag giggled in spite of the seriousness of the situation.

"So where do we start?"

"Well firstly," said Peter, "we need to find the keys."

It was Morag who eventually located them. They'd searched the kitchen from end to end and tried, unsuccesfully, to get into the housekeeper's rooms upstairs.

"If they're in there, we're sunk," Peter had said.

"Not necessarily," Morag had told him. "I'm an expert at lock-picking."

"You're kidding."

Morag took a hairpin from her pocket and waved it under his nose.

"Wouldn't be without it," she said. "My daddy's always losing his keys. Years of practice opening the medicine cabinet for him."

"You never cease to amaze me."

"You don't know the half of it," said Morag. "But we'd better explore all the other possibilities first."

The other possibilities included the library where Morag used her lock-picking skills to open the old writing desk in the corner.

And that's where they found them, in a small drawer at the back, under a mound of old bills dating back to the time of the elusive Mr Blane.

Peter picked them up with a whoop.

"Eureka," he shouted. "Morag, you're a genius." And he swept her up in a fierce hug, swinging her round till she was dizzy.

"Get off, you daft beggar." Morag swatted him until he let her down, her face pink with the compliment, or the hug, or both. "We'll need a torch," she said. "To see in the dark corners."

They fetched one from the kitchen and, after several attempts at finding the right key, unlocked the cellar door. Then they made their way gingerly down the stone steps into the heart of darkness.

The cellar was musty and damp. As with many old houses, built before the invention of damp-proof courses, electricity and central heating, it had been hollowed out of the earth, a storage space for seed potatoes and bottled fruit and shelter against the worst rigours of the Highland winter. In older times, when the snows came in, the entire household might move down until the thaw, bringing bedding, a box fire for heat and to cook on and a plentiful supply of candles. Underground, insulated from the bitter sub-arctic winds that could blow down the glen and take the skin off the bones, the family would be snug as a bug in a rug.

But on a day such as today, with the rain lashing against the granite, the water, seeping down through the walls, left the place damp and chill. And the single, unshaded bulb, swinging from the tacked on cable, did nothing to lighten the atmosphere.

The place was full of junk. An old mangle, tea-chests full of yellowing magazines, rusty garden tools, even an ancient sewing machine. The chaos only added to the sense of desolation and decay.

"Brrrr," Morag hugged herself. "Creepy."

Peter prodded one of the large flagstones that had been laid over the dirt to insulate the floor.

"Do you think she could have put him under one of those?"

Morag shook her head.

"They weigh a ton. You'd need two strong men and a couple of crowbars to make an impression on them. Mrs McNab's wiry but unless she had an accomplice she wouldn't have a hope."

They searched the cellar from end to end but there was no sign of anything that remotely resembled a place to hide a body. They peered into empty barrels, tapped the walls for possible hollows, emptied tea chests, even unrolled a moth-eaten rug in case, like Cleopatra on her first visit to Julius Caesar, the body had been secreted within its folds.

Nothing.

Eventually, chilled to the marrow and thoroughly worn out, they made their bedraggled way back upstairs, locking the door behind them.

Peter put the kettle on and dug out the biscuit barrel while Morag nipped up to the first floor to check on Johnny.

He was still out for the count.

So the two conspirators retired to the library to drown their disappointment in hot sweet tea and jammy dodgers.

"Well, we tried," said Morag.

"Much good it did us."

"I suppose we'd better put the keys back? Cover our tracks. Hide the evidence."

"I suppose."

Morag rose and crossed to the writing desk. She pulled out the drawer that had housed the keys. Too hard as it happens. It slid from its mooring and crashed to the floor scattering papers here, there and everywhere.

"Blast," she said.

"Butter-fingers," said Peter, rising to help her clear up the mess.

They knelt, side by side and, while Peter shuffled the papers into piles, Morag turned the upended drawer right way round again.

"Hey, look," she said.

"What?"

"There's something taped to the back here."

And, indeed, there was. A folded paper, faded with age, which, when they opened it, spreading it out on the carpet in front of them, proved to be a crude map of the layout of the house. All four floors from cellar to attic. The date said 1537. Two hundred years before Jeannie McClure had been burned at the stake.

"Why would they have hidden it?" Peter wanted to know, as they pored over the ancient drawing.

"Sometimes these old houses had secret passages and the like," said Morag. "They used to hide people in them. It started with religious persecutions. Priests and nuns would be hidden by the family from the Protestant backlash. Then, after the 1715 uprising when the English were on the rampage, they used them to hide men on the run. They did the same in England during the time of Cromwell and the Civil war down south."

"History was never my strong point," admitted Peter.

"Aye, well, maybe there's a hidey-hole in this house?"

She pointed at the map excitedly.

"Yes, look," she said. "Here, in the library, behind the far bookcase, there's a hollow and an arrow and a name. 'The Necromancer'."

Peter got up and walked across to the bookcase. Outside the weather had worsened and, although it was barely two in the afternoon, the sky was black as night.

"Put the light on, would you?" he said. "I can't see a thing."

Morag did as she was bid and moved over to join him, the ground-plan still in her hand.

"Yes, there it is. Look. On the fourth shelf up."

The book was second from the end in the row. It was obviously very old, bound in red leather with faded gold lettering. They could just make out the title. "The Necromancer".

Peter looked at Morag in excitement.

"Do you think...?" he said.

"There's only one way to find out. You'll have to do it. I'm not tall enough."

Peter reached up and gently pulled the book from its moorings. It moved forward, hinging downwards from the top like a lever. There was a brief hiatus, a pause when nothing occured. Then, with a great deal of creaking and groaning, the bookcase swung outwards to reveal a small, dark opening.

Hunter S. Blane had not died a peaceful death. His mummified remains, dressed for outdoors in anorak and balaclava, were in a kneeling position, nails torn from scrabbling at the heavy, sound-deadening insulation that backed the bookshelves. However much air the niche held, it had not been enough to sustain life for long. The skeletal features, dried flesh stretched tight over the bones, were etched with the agony of suffocation, blind eyes wide open in supplication, mouth drawn back in a desperate scream that no one would ever hear.

As Peter and Morag clutched each other in horror, the body pitched forward and landed in a heap at their feet.

18

"Yoo-hoo, I'm back."

Mrs McNab's stentorian tones echoed down the hallway, followed by the sound of the front door slamming.

Peter and Morag looked at each other.

What now?

Peter made an instant decision.

"Get him back in and close the bookcase," he hissed. "I'll try to stall her."

"What? Touch that?" Morag shuddered. "No way."

"Helloooo. Peter." Mrs McNab again.

"You'd better," warned Peter. "Unless you want us to be the next ones for the chop." And he darted out into the hall.

"Hello, Mrs McNab," he said. "I wasn't expecting you for ages yet."

The housekeeper was in the process of removing her raincoat, shaking it to get rid of some of the deluge that had almost soaked her on her way from car to house.

"Aye, well, the motorway was practically impassable," she said. "The rain is coming down in sheets, bouncing off the road windscreen high. I pulled into one of the service stations for a whiley to see if it would ease off. Had a bitey of lunch. But it just seemed to be getting worse. It was like trying to drive through a waterfall. So I decided not to chance it. How's he been?"

"Who?"

"Who? Johnny, of course. Have you not even looked in on the mite?"

"Of course, he's ... he's ... fine."

"Then why are you looking so guilty?"

Mrs McNab plonked her dripping umbrella in the stand and went to move past him. Peter moved sideways to block her way.

"Where are you going?"he asked.

"I'm going to the kitchen, if you don't mind, to make myself a cup of tea. I'm chilled to the marrow."

"Why don't you go on upstairs and get out of those wet things?" said Peter. "We don't want you to catch cold. I'll make some tea and bring it up to you. Would you like a biscuit?"

Mrs McNab narrowed her eyes.

"What's going on?" she said.

Peter tried to look innocent.

"Why should something be going on?" he said.

"Because normally you wouldn't care if I dropped dead in my shoes," she said. "Now suddenly you're all sweetness and light. And what were you doing in the library?"

"What?"

"You heard. The library. Have you been into my Blane's books again? "

She pushed past him and marched down the hallway.

Morag was standing with her back to the bookcase. Somehow she'd managed to get the late Mr Blane back into his hiding place and close the opening. Almost, but not quite. Peter could see that "The Necromancer" was tilted at a slight angle and that the bookcase wasn't quite shut. With luck Mrs McNab wouldn't notice.

The housekeeper stiffened.

"Ah, so that's it?" she said. "You here again, madam. Up to no good, I'll be bound."

"I only came over to keep him company." Morag was white as a sheet. She had a strong stomach but shoving the mortal remains of Hunter S. Blane back into his cubbyhole had been one of the most revolting things she'd ever had to do in her life.

"Doing what, if I may ask?" sneered Mrs McNab. "I'll bet you haven't been playing snakes and ladders."

Behind her, Morag could feel the bookcase pressing against her back. She hadn't quite managed to close it in time. Another second and it would have been done. The pressure increased. She wanted to run but she daren't move. The weight of the body was pushing it open again.

"My daddy dropped me off on his way to do his rounds," she said, lamely. "He'll be back to pick me up any minute."

"I should think so too," sniffed the housekeeper. "Your daddy's far too free and easy, dropping people off in other people's houses without so much as a by your leave."

"She had a by your leave," Peter said out loud, "I invited her."

Inside he was saying "Don't look up, don't look up," because behind Morag, on the fourth shelf up, "The Necromancer" was moving slowly down and out.

Morag leant backwards and closed her eyes. Her knees felt weak. She wished her daddy would turn up.

Mrs McNab took a step towards her, peering at the face, pallid beneath its dusting of freckles.

"You don't look well," she said.

Then she swung round to look at Peter. His expression was that of a rabbit mesmerized by the headlights of a car. He was looking up towards the wall behind Morag's head. He too, was pale as death.

"What ails the pair of you?" snarled Mrs McNab. "You look as though you've seen a ghost."

It was the noise that made her swing round again, the creaking as the mechanism moved the bookcase inexorably out, pushing Morag with it. Giving up the fight to hold it back, she rushed past the startled housekeeper and flung herself at Peter.

So once more they stood clasped in a tight huddle as the body of Hunter S. Blane fell out on the floor.

Whatever reaction Peter and Morag were expecting (glinting eyes and maniacal laughter – a sudden rush to the kitchen for carving knives), it was not the one they got.

As Mr Blane lay, curled in rigor mortis, screaming dumbly at the ceiling, there was a breath-held moment of complete and utter silence.

Then Mrs McNab, the stiff, the unbending, the hard-as-nails Mrs McNab, fell to her knees beside all that was left of her ex-employer and howled like an abandoned dog. Gathering the pathetic remains into her arms she promptly burst into tears.

"Oh Mr Blane," she sobbed. "Hunter. I thought sure the Bogle had got you. And here you were, all the time."

And this was how Dr Sutherland found her when he arrived to pick Morag up ten minutes later. Crosslegged on the carpet, the body clasped to her thin chest, rocking it like a dead baby.

It took him all of two seconds to sum up the situation, then he took charge.

"Morag," he said. "Go into the kitchen and make some tea. Peter, call the police."

Then gently disentangling her from the macabre bundle of flesh and bone, he led the distraught housekeeper to the sofa and bade her lie down.

19

After all the kerfuffle, the big, old building was quiet again, and Peter was once more on his own in the house with Johnny.

He sat at the table in the kitchen and stared out into the night while his brother continued to doze uptairs. The weather had deteriorated into a mini-hurricane. Gale-force winds and fierce driving sleet. The storm howled round the house like a banshee, bending the trees in the garden to breaking point and threatening to send the chimneys toppling through the roof.

Peter just hoped that the generator would hold out.

He took a bite of his cheese sandwich and a large gulp of milk and ran over the sequence of events of the past few hours in his head.

The police had come and gone, as had the

ambulance, which had removed the body to the mortuary where the post mortem would be held. Peter and Morag had been questioned on the spot but Mrs McNab had been asked to accompany the police to the station, to assist them with their enquiries. Purely a matter of routine, they had said, since the man had obviously got trapped in there by mistake. There would have to be an inquest, of course, but the local constabulary were of the firm opinion that a verdict of misadventure would be recorded. However, the proprieties had to be observed and Mrs McNab had been the last one to see the late Mr Blane alive.

Accordingly, the housekeeper had been whisked away in the panda, red-eyed and unnerved, to "answer a few questions". She looked so pathetic Peter even found himself feeling sorry for her.

And guilty.

After all the speculation, the whole thing had turned out to be nothing more than a load of malicious gossip. She hadn't murdered the late Mr Blane after all. And she certainly hadn't buried him in the cellar.

Instead it looked like Jeannie McClure's curse had claimed another victim.

Dr Sutherland had stayed behind long enough to give Johnny a thorough going-over before taking Morag home and driving down to the station to sign the papers recording his professional opinion on the probable cause of death. Suffocation.

Johnny had come round briefly to clasp the doctor by the arm and tell him that the Bogle was eating him up. Morag's father, using his best bedside manner, which Peter thought was considerable, had stroked the boy's forehead and told him not to worry and calmed him down enough to get an aspirin and some warm milk into him. Eventually, he'd fallen asleep again.

Peter had used the opportunity to go downstairs to the kitchen and make himself something to eat. He'd been on duty since early in the morning on what had proved an exceedingly eventful day. He hadn't had any lunch. He was exhausted and he was starving.

He was just wondering whether it was worth waiting up for Mrs McNab or whether he should just go on to bed when the scream came.

It was like nothing Peter had ever heard before. Or wished to hear again. Not Johnny's usual low moaning cry but a high-pitched shriek followed by a gurgling wail.

Peter took the stairs three at a time, bursting into Johnny's bedroom like a battering ram.

Johnny was backed up against the bed-head, his arms held straight out in front of him as if trying to hold something at bay. And this time it wasn't his imagination, this time there really was something there. Peter could see it too. A white mist hanging over the bed like a smothering cloud.

The Bogle was in the house with them.

Slowly, it began to descend, insinuating itself in and around Johnny's frail body while he continued to scream and howl and thrash and try to push himself into the wall.

Peter did the only thing he could think of. He grabbed Johnny's dressing-gown from its peg behind the door and began to swipe at the hovering apparition.

To his surprise, the Bogle retreated, rising halfway to the ceiling, hanging there in a sort of malignant limbo. It hesitated for a moment, as though at a loss to know what to do. Then it drifted slowly across the room and out through the window into the storm.

A huge bolt of lightning shot across the night sky, throwing the spectre into translucent relief as it traversed the garden and disappeared up the lane towards Crossmaglen.

Peter rushed to the window, heaved open the sash and stuck his head out, squinting his eyes against the sting of the storm.

But the Bogle had gone.

Slowly, he closed the window and turned back into the room. He was shaking like a leaf.

Johnny collapsed back against the pillows with a moan, eyes tight shut, lips moving wordlessly, fingers plucking at the bedclothes.

Peter looked at his brother helplessly. Could he have imagined it?

He looked at his watch. There were still twenty odd days to next dark of the moon. But no – he hadn't imagined it. The Bogle had been here. In this very room. Something had to be done. And soon.

Turning on his heel, he clattered downstairs to call Morag.

This was an emergency.

"Hey," she said. "I was just about to ring you. Daddy brought Mrs McNab back from the station with him. She was that upset he thought he'd better give her a sedative. She's in our spare room at the moment, dead to the world. Daddy says not to wait up. He'll bring her home in the morning."

"We've got to go back to see Jeannie," Peter tried not to sound as frantic as he felt.

"Calm down. What's the matter?"

"It's been here, Morag."

"What's been where? What are you talking about?"

"The Bogle, of course. I've just seen it. It was in Johnny's bedroom. I think it had come to feed."

"That's not possible," said Morag, an edge of fear creeping into her tone. "It only comes out at dark of the moon."

"I know that and you know that – but does the Bogle know that? Maybe it's changed the rules?"

"You haven't been ... dreaming about it, have you?"

"I have as it happens. How did you know?"

"I didn't," said Morag. "It's just that ... I have too."

165

"What's happening, Morag? If it can get into the house... If it can get into our heads..."

"You're right. We'll need to see Jeannie right away. She'll know what to do."

"I hope so."

"I hope so too. She's the only hope we've got. Get some rest. Provided the weather's cleared up we can go first thing. Here comes Daddy. Not a word."

And she hung up before he could even say "goodbye".

What followed was the longest night of Peter's life. He spent it sitting by Johnny's bed. He didn't dare go into his own room in case the Bogle came back. He kept dozing off and dreaming that it was there and waking up in a cold sweat. Once he even imagined the horrible fetid cloud oozing through the crack under the door, the ghost of the late lamented Hunter S. Blane emerging from the mist and demanding revenge for having been disturbed from his long sleep. He'd jolted back to consciousness, his pyjama top saturated.

To make matters worse, the storm, instead of abating, got even fiercer, thunder rattling the roof-tiles, lightning shooting across the sky like Jumping Jack Flash. A rogue bolt struck the newly-repaired generator and, at three o'clock in the morning all the lights went out again.

Peter was too tired and too spooked to go

stumbling about looking for candles. He was afraid of what he might meet on the stairs. So he just sat there, shivering in the darkness, holding Johnny's hand and wishing as he'd never wished before, for dawn and the daylight.

20

Mrs McNab arrived just after eight to find Peter draped across his brother's frail body. They were both sound asleep. Johnny had interlaced his fingers in Peter's hair and was hanging on like grim death.

The housekeeper disentangled them one by one and would have sent Peter to his bed but he insisted he had to get out of the house.

"I'm going for a ride to clear my head," he said, and for once she didn't argue or give him the third degree. All she did was insist he had something to eat before he set off.

It was a much subdued Mrs McNab whom the doctor had dropped off that morning, her eyes red-rimmed with weeping, her face drawn with strain.

The police had discovered a diary on the body, she told Peter over breakfast, tucked into the inside pocket of the tweed jacket Mr Blane had been wearing under his anorak. In it were recorded the events of his last evening alive.

The entry said that not only was he convinced that the house was, indeed, cursed, (which was his main reason for moving on), but his researches had led him to believe that the entity known as the Death Bogle did, in fact, exist. However, unless he could see it first hand, perhaps record it on camera, he could not prove it to the world at large. Since tonight was dark of the moon he intended leaving a note for Mrs McNab, who didn't approve of him taking such risks, and making his way to the crossroads to see for himself. His housekeeper was at a whist drive, the diary stated, and by the time she came back, which she would do well before midnight, he would already be at Crossmaglen.

There was a postscript. He had just come across something very very interesting, it said, about a secret hiding place in the library. He was just going to check it out before he left.

"There's no catch on the inside," said Mrs McNab, tearfully. "The bookcase must have swung to on him. Once he was in, he couldnae get out."

Whether or not the late Hunter S. Blane had mentioned his trip to the doctor's earlier in the evening and his suspicions that someone might be poisoning him, Mrs McNab didn't say. And Peter didn't ask. The woman was upset enough as it was.

"To think of it," she said. "Him locked in there. And me in the house all the time." Her face crumpled and she buried it in her apron, shoulders heaving. "Poor Mr Blane."

Peter left his burnt toast and lukewarm coffee to comfort her and make his apologies.

"I'm really sorry, Mrs McNab," he said, putting a tentative hand on her shoulder.

"And to be taken away in a police car," sobbed the housekeeper. "Like a common criminal. The shame of it."

"I'm really, really sorry," said Peter again. "For thinking that you had anything to do with it."

"Aye, well." Mrs McNab, dried her eyes, pulling herself together. "At least it'll stop all the gossip. At least now they'll know I didn't murder him and bury him in the cellar."

"Can I get you anything?" said Peter. "Would you like me to stay with you for a while?"

Mrs McNab shook her head.

"No, away on out with you," she said. "It's a fine morning. The fresh air will do you good. You were on duty all day yesterday. Fair's fair. I'll look after the bairn."

She managed a watery smile.

Peter couldn't remember her ever having smiled at him before.

He smiled back. Then he leant forward and gave her a quick peck on the cheek. The housekeeper stiffened in astonishment.

"Thanks Mrs McNab," he said and then, as an afterthought, and before he hurried out, "By the way, the generator's gone again."

Mrs McNab put her hand up to where he had kissed her and sighed.

"Welcome home," she said under her breath. Then she went off in search of the mobile with which to call the electrician.

"She's a changed woman," Peter told Jeannie, when he and Morag arrived at the cottage an hour or so later. "It turns out she didn't do it after all."

"I could have told you that," said Jeannie, pouring tea. "Malicious gossip. The eighth deadly sin. You should hear some of the things they say about me. A couple of hundred years ago I'd have been incinerated for half of them."

"Like the other Jeannie," said Morag.

"Indeed," said the witchwoman. "But if they've a sick cow that the vet can't cure or if they want a love potion or a good-luck charm, they'll still come to me."

"So you DO have the power?" said Peter.

"Oh, I have it, all right. But power brings responsibility. You have to be careful how you use it or it'll turn round and bite you. Power used for evil always comes back on the evildoer."

"Cause and effect," said Morag.

"Precisely," said Jeannie. "And now, to what do I owe the pleasure of this visit? I take it you didn't do that climb for the good of your health?"

"Peter's seen the Bogle," said Morag, coming straight to the point.

The witchwoman's hand went involuntarily to her throat. A small bronze amulet that hung there, in the shape of a six-pointed star with a crescent moon at its centre.

"Where?" she asked.

"In Johnny's bedroom," said Peter. "Hanging over the bed. Scared the wits out of me. I swatted it with his dressing-gown," he added, "and it floated off out of the window."

"You were lucky," said Jeannie. "It musn't have been too hungry."

"Johnny was petrified," said Peter. "You've never heard such screaming." He shuddered at the memory.

"It was Johnny that brought it," said Jeannie. "And out of it's time. This is more serious than I thought. Tell me. Have either of you been dreaming about it?"

"Both of us," said Morag. "Does that mean anything?"

"I'm afraid it means that it has the pair of you marked down as its next victims."

"But I thought it only came out at dark of the moon?" said Peter. "If that's the case, how CAN I have seen it. Are we not safe in our beds any more?"

"It has always been predicted," said the witchwoman, "that when the Bogle had gathered enough evil into itself it would be able to break free

172

from the confines of time and space and roam unhindered anywhere it pleases." She looked at Peter and Morag seriously. "It looks like we may have come to that point."

"So if it can get free whenever it likes – could we raise it?" blurted Peter.

Jeannie looked at him curiously. Morag stared at him in astonishment. Ariel raised his orange hackles and hissed at such a suggestion.

"Why would you want to do that?"

"We need to face it sometime," he said. "The longer we leave it, the stronger it gets. And the stronger it gets, the weaker Johnny gets. You said you could do something next dark of the moon. Can we raise the Bogle before that?" He took a deep breath before he spoke again. "If you used me as bait," he said.

The witchwoman appraised him with her clear, grey eyes.

"You'd be taking a terrible chance," she told him.

"I'll be taking a chance when the time comes anyway, won't I? If we can take it on the hop, raise it and face it when it's not expecting us, would we not have some advantage at least?"

"There's that, I suppose," said Jeannie.

"If I have to wait until dark of the moon I'll be a nervous wreck. And the Bogle will be two weeks the stronger. Better to get it over and done with now."

Morag put out a hand and squeezed his shoulder.

"You're awful brave," she said, admiringly.

"Not a bit of it," said Peter, unwilling to take credit where it wasn't due. "If you want to know, I'm scared to death. But I'm the one that got Johnny into this. It's only right that I should try to get him out."

"Then I'll come with you," said Morag. "I'm as much to blame as you are,"

"You don't have to."

"I know. But what kind of friend would let you face that thing on your own? Two heads are better than one – eh, Jeannie?"

"I suppose. As long as you don't distract each other." The witchwoman hesitated, then came to a decision. "Very well," she said, "We can try."

"When?"

"The sooner the better. Tomorrow night. I'll need to consult my reference books and the cards. Luckily I've already done some work on the ritual in advance. But I'll need to prepare a potion and energize a spell. And then you'll both be wanting amulets." She touched the charm at her throat again. "For extra protection. Come back tomorrow evening," she said finally. "I should have something ready for you by then."

"Tomorrow?" said Peter, thinking of the trek up the hill. "Can't you do something now?"

The witchwoman raised her eyebrows and glared balefully at him.

"Conjuring up an entity like the Bogle and then

doing away with it is a bittie more complicated than boiling an egg," she said. "It'll take me all of today, the best part of the night and most of tomorrow morning to come up with something strong enough. Unless you'd like me to send you in against that thing half prepared?"

She paused, waiting for a response. Morag kicked Peter under the table.

"Sorry," he mumbled.

"Before you go," said Jeannie, rising and taking a book down from one of her pine polished shelves. "I'd like you to hear something."

She turned to a page that had been marked with a strip of woven cloth and began to read.

"In the year of Our Lord 1326, Kirstie McBride, handmaiden of Satan and several lesser-known Devils, did, with the aid of various diabolical spells and occult incantations and, in the company of her familiar, a black toad known as Beelzebub that suckled at her breast, successfully raise the Death Bogle outwith its designated hour of midnight at dark of the moon.

Jeannie turned the page and continued...

"Her familiar, her house and all its contents, including herself, were then consumed by fire which raged for a half month, nobody being able to put it out. Accordingly all trace of the said Kirstie McBride was reduced to ashes finer than the finest sand and blown away on the wind."

She shut the book with a snap.

"Just thought you ought to know what we're letting ourselves in for," she said. "Now get off home, the both of you. And be sure to get some sleep tonight. You'll not be getting much tomorrow evening, I'm thinking."

21

The first thing Peter noticed when they arrived the following afternoon was that the furniture had been rearranged. Everything had been pushed back against the walls and a bright red pentacle had been painted on the floor. There was an acrid smell, like sulphur, in the air and Ariel lay curled on the rocking-chair, fast asleep.

In the centre of the table lay various items – a couple of charms on leather thongs, similar to the one worn by Jeannie, a sheet of paper on which were printed several lines of archaic script and a small blue bottle stoppered with a cork.

The witchwoman solemnly hung the charms round Peter and Morag's necks, then set them both down with a glass of elderberry cordial to explain the plan.

"I decided that a simple spell wouldn't be strong

enough," she said "So I've prepared a ritual with a force of three."

"Three is a very powerful magic number," said Morag under her breath.

"The first part is in the form of a chant," Jeannie went on. "Words bring thoughts in from the ether and make them concrete. They are a very effective force for good."

"Or evil?" suggested Peter.

"Or evil," Jeannie agreed. "But luckily the Bogle cannae speak. It's one of the few advantages we have and we might as well make the most of it."

"What's in the bottle?" Morag's curiosity got the better of her.

"Preserve yourself in patience and stop interrupting me and you might find out," said Jeannie.

She picked up the small blue bottle and held it to the light. A rogue sunbeam, glancing off the glass, sparkled in its depths like a sapphire.

"It's a potion," she said, "made from purest spring water and a mixture of other ingredients that needn't concern you. Water is one of the greatest solvents in the world. If you dig an old piece of crockery out of the earth, encrusted with dirt, it would take you a month to scrape it off. But if you leave it under running water, it'll be clean in five minutes. So it stands to reason that water can also wash away any other foul thing."

"And is this the third part of the ritual?" Peter fingered the charm at his throat.

The witchwoman shook her head.

"No, that's only an extra bit of insurance," she said. "The third part is a sign. And it's the most important part so you'll need to get it right. It's an ancient configuration designed to ward off evil and it's very specific. If you do not place the hands correctly, it willnae work. If you do it correctly, it will protect you and keep the creature at bay while the other two items take effect. Now watch carefully and do exactly as I do."

Holding up the forefinger and thumb of her left hand she brought them together to form them into the shape of an eye. Then she placed the palm of her other hand against the aperture, facing away from her. The pentacle tattooed on her palm winked through the space.

"Is that it?" said Peter, after he and Morag had practised the position several times to make sure they'd got it exactly right.

"It is. But I must draw a pentacle on each of your palms to complete the effect."

And she proceeded to do so using, of all things, a magic marker.

"Be careful you don't get it wet," she said. "We don't want the lines to go fuzzy. And remember to hold the hands directly across your own eyes so as not to confuse the issue. Eyes are a soft, vulnerable part of the body, much less tough than skin. And the Bogle has powerful hypnotic powers. If it enters through your eyes, you are lost."

Peter shivered, remembering what Morag had told him about corbies going for the eyes on dead bodies first.

"One last thing," said the witchwoman. "You MUST use all three parts of the ritual. No single item is effective enough of itself to halt the Bogle in its tracks. Dinnae forget. Since Morag has volunteered to go along, I suggest that one of you chants the spell while the other one throws the potion. You must get close enough to make sure that your aim is good. None of it must be wasted. Use the holding sign to protect you while you move in and then immediately afterwards for protection while the ritual does its work. Is that clear?"

Peter was beginning to think that the whole thing was ridiculous. Spells and potions indeed. He looked round the room at the herb pots and the crystal ball and the orange cat whose fur so exactly matched Morag's wild hair. He couldn't believe this was happening. It was like something out of the Middle Ages. Even though he had started the whole thing, only the serious look on his friend's face stopped him from calling a halt to the entire episode then and there.

That, and the memory of Johnny, wasting away in the big old house further down the glen.

A house with a curse on it.

"I'll take the potion," Morag held out her hand.

"Better not. The person with the potion will have to get closest to the Bogle," said Jeannie. "Peter's the tallest. He'll have the longest throw. And he's the strongest. And oldest. It's only fair that he should take the biggest risk."

She looked expectantly at Peter and he reached for the bottle. It felt cool against his palm. Morag picked up the spell, folded it and tucked it in the pocket of her shorts.

The witchwoman nodded her approval.

"Speak the words loud and clear," she said. "You have a good, carrying voice, Morag. Try to keep any shake out of it when the time comes."

She stood and ushered them to the door.

"Now, if you'll excuse me," she said. "I'll need to be catching up on my sleep. I didn't get a wink last night. One more thing," she added, as they all trooped outside. "You'll need to take the boy with you."

"Johnny?" exclaimed Peter. "But that's impossible."

"It's imperative," said the witchwoman, firmly. "If he's not present the mark cannot be erased."

"But how am I supposed to get him there?" Peter protested. "I can't drive and I certainly can't take him on my bike."

"If necessary you'll have to carry him. You're a big, strong lad and the poor mite is probably all skin and bone by now."

"Couldn't you give us a lift?"

"I will need to stay up here," said Jeannie. "I'll

be conjuring up the Bogle remember? I'll need various bits of paraphernalia about me to do that. Things that can't be carried. Things," she added, mysteriously, "that shouldn't be seen. Anyway, too many bodies on site would just complicate matters. If it's any consolation, I shall be with you in spirit and overseeing the proceedings through my crystal. Now off you go – and good luck."

"They'll need it," she added quietly to the big ginger cat which had just joined her in the doorway. She knelt down and picked the heavy animal up, scratching him gently behind the ears. "Come on, Ariel, just time for a nap before the battle commences."

22

Peter stared down at his younger brother. The witchwoman had been right, Johnny was reduced to nothing but skin and bone. Another two weeks and there'd be nothing left to resurrect. The mark had spread right over his forehead and up into his hairline. And everywhere it touched, the hair had dropped out in clumps. Gone was the long silky fringe that used to be for ever falling in his eyes. He was almost bald. He looked like a little old man.

It was ten-thirty and time to go. Peter slid his hands under his brother's neck and knees. Gently, so as not to wake him. Mrs McNab had been fussing over him like a mother hen all day as though, by being extra nice to him, she could make up for what had happened to "poor Mr Blane". A mere squeak from Johnny might have her downstairs again. The last thing Peter wanted.

He had arranged to met Morag at the crossroads at eleven forty-five. On foot it would take him much longer than it had done on his bike.

The weather was foul, clammy and warm – a paradise for midges. A grey-green mist hung just above the heather making it impossible to see whether one was treading on solid ground or about to fall into a hole. Peter hoped he wouldn't rick his ankle on the way. Tonight of all nights, he couldn't afford to be late.

He looked around for something to wrap Johnny in. Something not too warm but that would bind him securely enough to stop his legs and arms from flailing about. He decided that the sheet was as good as anything. When he wound the white cloth around his brother it looked uncomfortably like a shroud. But Johnny didn't stir. He just lay there, like a dead thing, while Peter lifted him clear of the bed.

He was as light as a feather.

"It's an ill wind," thought Peter.

The journey wasn't going to be as tiring as he'd anticipated.

Meanwhile, over at the Sutherland house, Morag was making her own preparations.

Her father normally didn't go to bed until well after midnight, so she decided she'd better hurry things along a bit.

At ten-thirty, she made a cup of Horlicks and

took it in to where he was happily dozing in front of the TV.

"You look beat, Daddy," she said, switching the set off. "Why don't you have an early night?"

"Hey," said her father. "I was watching that."

"I'll give you 50p if you can even tell me what programme it was," grinned Morag.

"You're being very considerate all of a sudden," the doctor tried another tack. "What's the catch?"

Morag tried, not very successfully, to look innocent.

"Does there have to be a catch?" she said. "You work too hard, is all. Somebody's got to look out for your welfare."

Dr Sutherland struggled to his feet.

"Well, maybe you're right," he said. "I have had a bit of a hard day."

He leaned over to kiss his daughter's upturned cheek.

"Night, sweetheart," he said. "Don't stay up too late."

"Night, Daddy." Morag gave him her best smile. "Sweet dreams."

Dr Sutherland disappeared out into the hall clutching his mug of Horlicks to his chest.

"I hope this isn't going to cost me in the morning," his voice echoed down from the stairwell. "But I have a sneaky feeling that it might."

*   *   *

185

Peter laid Johnny back on the bed and cursed himself for his own stupidity. He'd been out of the house and halfway up the lane before he realized that he'd forgotten the potion.

He dug it out of the back of the drawer where he'd secreted it earlier on and stuck it in the pocket of his jeans. Then he lifted Johnny up again. Light as his brother was, Peter could already feel the pull in the muscles of his shoulders and upper back.

He'd lost at least ten minutes and added an extra quarter of a mile to his journey by not concentrating in the first place.

What an idiot he was. He'd managed to sneak out once without Mrs McNab hearing him. Fingers crossed he could do it again.

He tiptoed downstairs, counting the treads so he could miss the squeaky one halfway down that he'd forgotten about first time around. Almost there. Just the hall to navigate – taking care not to bump into anything in the dark. Then they'd be free and clear.

Johnny stirred, struggling in his wrapping, opening his eyes to look at Peter.

"Where we going?" he said, quite lucidly. Quite loudly too.

Peter stopped in his tracks.

"Shhhhhh," he said. "It's a secret."

"A secret," said Johnny and then, sinking once more into a half-doze. "A secret ... a secre ... a sec..."

Peter cocked an ear to make sure there was no noise from the direction of the top landing.

All was silence.

With a sigh of relief he continued on his journey, past the library into the hall, across the tiled vestibule to the front door.

He was just opening it for the second time when he suddenly heard the car. Peering through the crack he was horrified to see the headlights of his dad's BMW swing into the forecourt.

Morag got out her bike and began to pedal steadily towards the crossroads at Crossmaglen, repeating the spell that she'd memorized by heart in case she lost the paper or it was too dark to read from it when the crunch came. No time to be fiddling round with torches when you were confronted by a demon from the depths intent on sucking out your soul!

She shivered.

What had she got herself into?

Why hadn't she let Peter do his own dirty work? As he'd said, it was his fight. She needn't have got involved at all.

But even as she thought it, she knew this wasn't true. It was easy to be a friend when everything was going well. But a *real* friend was someone who stood by you when the going got rough.

The crossroads hove into view. She looked at her watch.

Eleven-fifteen.

She was early.

She decided she wouldn't go any further until Peter arrived. She considered whether she should cycle towards his house and meet him but then thought better of it. There was just a chance he might take another route and they'd miss each other.

Best stay where she was.

She got off her bike and sat down by the side of the road, wondering how Peter was managing on foot, carrying Johnny.

And just how far he'd got?

Peter had only got as far as halfway back down the hall when his dad opened the front door and caught him red-handed.

He'd been making for the library in a panic. If he could hide in there until his dad went to bed, he reasoned – assuming, since the house was in darkness, that they were all fast asleep – then he might still make it. Taken on the hop, it was the best he could do.

In the event, he wasn't quite quick enough.

When Mark Wilson turned on the light, Peter was just turning in through the library door. Johnny, dangling in his arms, woke up suddenly and began to whimper.

"What the hell are you up to?" His dad looked as taken aback as Peter was. "And what are you doing with Johnny?"

*   *   *

Morag looked at her watch again.

She felt as though she'd been waiting at the roadside since early childhood.

She'd kept the night terrors at bay by practising the sign and chanting the spell until its rhythms and rhymes buzzed inside her head like a demented bee.

Peter was cutting it a bit fine. Only ten minutes to go.

She repeated the incantation over and over like a mantra, to keep her mind off what she knew would be materializing very soon. The amulet that Jeannie had given her felt cool and comforting against her skin. Insurance, the witchwoman had said. She hoped it was life insurance.

She decided that if Peter hadn't arrived in the next five minutes she would get out of there. She was certain he wouldn't deliberately let her down. If he didn't turn up something would have happened to prevent him getting here.

But friend or not, she had no intention of facing the Bogle alone. With only half a spell to her credit.

Five minutes – and then she'd leave.

What she didn't realize was that the battery on her Swatch was running down.

It was exactly four minutes slow.

"Are you crazy? Are you trying to kill him or what?" Mark Wilson was practically foaming at the mouth. "Give him to me this instant."

He tried to take Johnny out of Peter's arms. But Peter wouldn't let go. He backed away until the wall prevented him from going any further. After that an unseemly tug-of-war began with poor Johnny wailing in the middle.

At this point, Mrs McNab arrived at the top of the stairs in a flannelette nightie and a hairnet. She looked about as appetizing as a cold rice pudding.

"Mr Wilson," she said, snatching off the net and trying to shake out her hair. "Why are you back so soon? And what's Johnny doing out of bed?"

"You may well ask," said Mr Wilson, grimly. "As for being back, I'm here because I've got the sack."

There was a stunned silence. Then Johnny pointed towards the front door and started to scream.

"The Bogle. The Bogle's coming."

Mr Wilson wrestled Johnny out of Peter's clutches.

"Get upstairs," he said, furiously. "Before I REALLY lose my temper."

"The Bogle," screamed Johnny. "It's coming to get us all."

Peter thought about Morag, all alone at Crossmaglen crossroads with only a piece of paper between her and Armageddon. He reached for his brother, trying to grab him back.

"Please Dad," he said, urgently. "I can't explain now but I've got to get Johnny to the crossroads by midnight."

"And what I've got to do is get Johnny back to bed right now."

"But Dad, you don't understand." Peter knew it was hopeless but he had to give it one last shot. It was too late to get there on foot. But maybe he could get his dad to drive him?

"This is a matter of life and death," he persisted. "Please. It's nearly twelve. Morag will be out there all on her own."

"So it's Morag again, is it?" shrilled Mrs McNab, relapsing into her old intransigent self. "That girl ought to be locked up. She's a menace to the community."

Mark Wilson brushed past Peter and began to carry a still-howling Johnny past the housekeeper and up the stairs.

This time Peter didn't resist. Instead he turned and raced for the door.

It was too late to save his brother.

But at least he could try to save his friend.

Up in the cottage at the top of Ben Croicht, Jeannie McClure felt a cold wind envelop her. She straightened up from where she'd been crouching over the crystal globe, concentrating her considerable psychic power on the struggle that was about to start down at Crossmaglen.

She had done her part. She had raised the Bogle. She could feel its evil presence stirring just below the realms of reality. Any moment now it would

191

emerge from its lair. Nothing could stop it. It had scented prey.

The rest was up to Peter and Morag.

But something had gone terribly wrong. Her bones protested with the certainty of it. What could it be? She thought she'd covered every eventuality.

Apparently not.

Morag was in mortal danger.

Rushing out of the door with Ariel at her heels, she leapt into her truck and gunned the motor to life. Jars and baskets clattered about in the back as she barrelled off in the direction of the crossroads.

But she was still only halfway down the hill when the church bell chimed midnight and she knew, with a hollow feeling in the pit of her stomach, that she was already too late.

Peter heard it too. He'd retrieved his bike from the garage and was riding hell for leather towards the rendezvous when it sounded in his ears like the knell of doom.

Behind him, he could hear his father shouting for him to "get back here at once". But he took no notice. Even when he heard the car start and take off after him, he still kept going. This can't be happening, he kept thinking, it can't be happening.

But it was.

Morag had just picked up her bike when the bell tolled. She figured Peter must have chickened out at the last minute and she was about to make herself scarce.

As the sudden, icy blanket of freezing air descended on the crossroads, she looked uncomprehendingly at her watch. It said four minutes to.

Morag didn't know how, or why, it had happened. It shouldn't have happened. It couldn't have happened.

But the awful truth was – it was midnight, she was all alone – and her number was about to come up.

23

Everybody converged on the crossroads at once. Peter on his bike. Mark Wilson in the BMW. Jeannie McClure in her psychedelic van.

Much good it did any of them – least of all Morag.

The damage had already been done.

She lay like a broken doll in the lee of the standing stone, her fallen bicycle discarded some metres away, its front wheel spinning forlornly as though propelled by some unseen force.

Jeannie was the first one to spot her. Turning off the engine, she scrambled from the van and ran over to kneel by the girl's body.

Peter was close behind. Hurling his bike on top of Morag's, he pushed the witchwoman aside and grabbed his friend by the shoulders, raising her upper body off the ground.

Her head lolled backwards, the freckles standing out stark against her blood-drained face. The unruly red mane fell back from her forehead. There, planted right in the centre, was a livid mark identical to Johnny's.

The cry that leapt from Peter's throat was almost as loud as the Bogle's howl of triumph had been. It held all the anguish and grief which he had felt, but never been able to express, after the loss of his mother.

Mark Wilson strode over from his car.

"What is it? What's going on?"

Peter ignored him, pulling Morag's head into his chest, burying his face in her hair. Instead, the witchwoman rose to meet him.

"I am Jeannie McClure," she introduced herself. "And you will be Peter's father."

"I told you," Peter looked up from where he was still cradling Morag in his arms. The hate in his eyes struck his father like a blow. "I told you she was in danger. But you just wouldn't listen. Why do you NEVER listen?"

His dad, torn between anger and bewilderment, turned to the witchwoman for an explanation.

"I don't understand," he said. "What's happened here?"

But Jeannie said nothing. She just continued to look down sadly at Peter and the unconscious girl. Mr Wilson followed her gaze, spotted the mark, blanched.

"Good God," he said, under his breath.

"He wouldn't let me come." Peter spoke about his dad, as though he wasn't there, directing his conversation to the witchwoman, trying to explain. "I forgot the potion and had to go back. I was on the way – with Johnny – when he arrived and spoiled it all."

Jeannie laid a calming hand on Peter's shoulder, trying to alleviate his obvious distress.

"It's all right," she said. "I know it wasn't your fault."

"But it's not all right," said Peter "It's not all right. First Johnny, now Morag. It *is* my fault. I started it and it IS my fault."

"Will somebody PLEASE tell me what's going on?" demanded his dad.

"The Bogle's got her. That's what's going on," shouted Peter. "If you hadn't come back and messed it all up, everything would be fixed by now."

"You're ranting, Peter," his dad yelled back. "There's no such thing as the Bogle. It's a legend. A fairy tale invented to scare small children into behaving themselves."

"Then what did this?" Peter wanted to know.

"I don't know. The same thing that did it to Johnny, obviously." He leant over to touch Morag's forehead. "It looks like some kind of a bite. A snake." He looked up at the witchwoman. "Are there snakes in these mountains? You're an adult. Give me an informed guess, at least."

But Jeannie refused to be drawn.

"Maybe something's escaped from the zoo?" said Mr Wilson. "That howl – you must have heard it. Or a poisonous spider. That's it! Something that arrived from abroad in a bunch of bananas."

"And walked all the way from the Glasgow docks?" said Peter, his voice heavily larded with sarcasm. "Highly likely."

"This is no time to be having an arguement," Jeannie's steady tones cut in on the raised voices. "We need to be getting Morag back to her father's house."

Mr Wilson looked at her suspiciously.

"What's your interest in all this?" he said. "What are you doing here anyway?"

Peter was about to say something but Jeannie stopped him with a warning look.

"I might ask the same of you," she said, gently.

"You're the one Mrs McNab calls the witchwoman."

It was almost an accusation. But Jeannie just smiled.

"Will you take her – or shall I?" she said.

"I'll take her." Mark Wilson bent to lift Morag up.

Peter shrugged him away.

"I'll take her," he said, fiercely. "She's my responsibility." And he stood up, staggering slightly. Morag, although slim, was all muscle and no mean weight. "Can we use your van, Jeannie?"

"I think maybe it's best that you go with your father," said Jeannie.

"Whatever you say."

Peter turned and walked reluctantly towards the BMW. Mark Wilson followed on and opened the back door.

As Peter slid Morag into the back seat and climbed in beside her, she stirred, opening her eyes groggily. Then memory flooded back and she grasped Peter by the arm, clinging to him like a limpet.

"Late," she said. "You were late."

"I know. I couldn't help it."

Morag's face contracted into a spasm of pure terror.

"Don't leave me," she said.

Then she sank back against the leather of the seats, lids closing over the distress in her eyes.

"I won't leave you," said Peter, hugging her tight. "Don't worry."

Mark Wilson closed the car door on them and turned back to confront the witchwoman.

"I don't know what part you play in all this," he said. "But if your mumbo-jumbo has been in any way responsible for Johnny's or this girl's condition, be assured that I will personally see to it that you answer for it under the full force of the law."

"It may have escaped your notice, Mr Wilson," Jeannie replied, coolly, "but the Spanish Inquisition was abolished some time ago."

"Come on," Peter shouted from the back of the car.

But Mark Wilson couldn't resist a parting shot.

"Mrs McNab was right," he said, his face flushed with anger. "People like you ought to be locked up."

Jeannie looked at him sadly.

"I pity you," she said. "I know you mean well. I sympathize with your problems and I forgive your ignorance. But your son is already twice the man that you will ever be. And I have to tell you now that you have done more harm this night than you will ever know."

24

They were coming back out of the doctor's house when Peter spotted the fire on the mountain.

His father and Jeannie had parted on bad terms, him shaking his fist and shouting that there ought to be a law, her powering off up the hill to the cottage in a cloud of exhaust fumes, leaving them to transport Morag back home.

Dr Sutherland, woken out of his sleep, had at first been dazed, then concerned and finally, when he saw the mark, furious. Mark Wilson had wanted to talk but the doctor had dismissed him curtly, telling him the middle of the night was no time for discussions. He had allowed Peter to carry Morag up to her bedroom before ordering them off the premises like plague carriers and shutting the door in their faces.

At first Peter thought the glow in the sky was from the first rays of the rising sun, then he remembered Kirstie McBride, handmaiden of Satan and several lesser known devils, and the breath caught in his throat.

"Jeannie," he whispered.

Mark Wilson compressed his lips. "Don't mention that woman's name to me," he said, bitterly.

"No. Look." Peter pointed to the High Hills, to the red stain on the night sky. "Her house. Jeannie's house is on fire."

His dad turned to follow Peter's outstretched arm. Above on the mountain ridge banks of scarlet leapt against the darkness like a bloodsoaked parody of the famous Northen Lights. And within the striations of smoke and flame, just for an instant, Mr Wilson could have sworn he saw a deeper, darker gradation. As though some monstrous amorphous cloud was dancing, swaying in rhythm with the crackling flames.

Peter saw it too.

"The Bogle," he said, hoarsely. "It's taking its revenge."

Mark Wilson, troubleshooter, shook the fanciful image of the malevolent cloud away and was suddenly all business. Emergencies were his forte. This was something he was used to, something he could deal with. He rounded on his son.

"Where's the mobile?" he snapped.

"In the kitchen drawer," said Peter, "where it usually is. Anyway, Jeannie doesn't have a phone."

"I don't want to call Jeannie," said Mr Wilson, "I want to call the fire brigade."

He turned to hammer on the door, didn't stop until the doctor appeared, bleary-eyed and rumpled.

"What is it?" he demanded. "What do you want?"

"There's a fire on the mountain," said Peter. "It's the witchwoman's cottage. It's alight."

The doctor looked up at the spreading glow.

"Good God," he said. "What next?"

"Call the fire brigade," Mark Wilson barked and, as the doctor turned back into the house, "Peter, do you know the way?"

"I think so."

"Then let's go," and he raced to the BMW and leapt in, his son hot on his heels.

But by the time they arrived at the top of the pass, having taken a couple of wrong turns on the way, Jeannie's cottage was no more than a smouldering wreck. The evil-smelling cloud that Mark Wilson had spotted from down in the valley had disappeared. But despite the recent conflagration, there was a chill in the air that sent shivers down the spine.

Jeannie herself, clothes torn, face soot-smudged, hair like a dishevelled bird's nest, was scrabbling frantically among the blackened door posts. Except for a few superficial burns on hands and face, she appeared to be physically unhurt. But unlike her usual calm, collected self, she seemed close to hysteria.

"It's Ariel," she said, desperately. "I can't find him. I was coming over the hill, when the whole thing exploded. I can't find him anywhere. Ariel. Ariel."

Peter thought of Beelzebub, Kirstie McBride's toad, burned to a crisp in a fire that no one had been able to put out.

"Ariel?" said his dad.

"Her cat," said Peter and then, "There he is," for he had just spotted the big ginger tom cowering behind a clump of heather. His fur was singed and his whiskers had disappeared but he seemed to be otherwise intact.

Jeannie rushed round the scorched building and scooped him up in her arms. Burying her head in his pelt she hugged him to her chest in relief.

"I thought I'd lost you," she said.

"You've lost just about everything else," observed Peter's dad, looking round the charred wreckage. Flames were still licking some parts of the building, dying down and then flickering back to life as they found some other item to devour.

Jeannie looked up from where she was cradling the cat.

"Seven generations of McClure women have lived in that cottage," she said. "But there's not a single item in there that I would have traded for

Ariel. Stones can be replaced. Walls can be rebuilt. But the gift of life is the most precious thing we have. Once gone, it can never be replaced."

"Lucky you were out," said Mr Wilson. "The cat's not the only thing that might have lost its life. How did it start anyway? Did you leave the gas on, a fire burning, what?"

Jeannie shook her head.

"I have no gas. And who would have a fire on in this weather? No. I fear this was started deliberately."

"By whom?" said Mark Wilson.

Jeannie and Peter exchanged glances.

"Some poor soul that knows no better," said the witchwoman, her words warning Peter not to commit himself. "There's still a lot of ignorance about."

"But all your books, Jeannie," said Peter.

"Aye, they're a loss, all right."

"And your herbs. And all your stock for the fair."

"Herbs I can grow more of. And stock is just stuff."

A sharp breeze, vicious as it was unexpected, suddenly encouraged the smouldering embers of the ruined building into a line of fire that darted without warning past the peripheral wall of cottage and garden and out on to the main body of the mountain. Once there, it caught the heather with a whoof of glee and headed off down the hill, devouring everything in its path.

"Do you have a well?" Mark Wilson was instantly practical. "The fire brigade should be on its way, but they'll need a source of water."

As if on cue the double note of the siren could be heard heading up the hill.

"In the back," Jeannie got to her feet to lead the way. "There's a bucket on a rope."

"It's a start. I'll take that, you and Peter see if you can find anything else that will still hold water."

But before they could even begin the impossible job of trying to contain a runaway fire with a single bucket and a couple of blackened saucepans, the professionals had powered into the clearing to tackle the conflagration with more appropriate tools.

The three stood aside and watched the firemen gradually bring the problem under control.

"It's a pity they didn't have hoses in Kirstie McBride's time," observed Peter.

Jeannie smiled wanly. Now that it was all over she had begun to shake. Mark Wilson, recognizing delayed shock, removed his jacket and wrapped it round her shoulders.

"What will you do now?" he said.

"Rebuild. I cannot let a thing like this force me out."

"I mean immediately. Is there somewhere you can go? Someone who would give you a bed?"

"Around Drumnadrochit," Jeannie smiled mirthlessly. "I doubt not. They think I have the evil eye. They will not wish it brought under their roof."

"You could move into our house for the time being," Peter butted in. "You don't believe in the evil eye, do you, Dad?"

"I don't think..." Jeannie began.

"She could, couldn't she Dad?" Peter interrupted her. "We've got loads of rooms we're not using."

"That's true. Though I can't think what Mrs McNab would have to say about it."

"Jeannie could lend a hand with Johnny. Give Mrs McNab a break. Give us all a break. You wouldn't mind doing that, would you Jeannie?"

"Of course not. But I don't think it would make your dad very popular. I'm not exactly Mrs McNab's favourite person, remember?"

Peter had a sudden brainwave.

"But it would lift the curse," he said. "A McClure living under the roof would lift the curse."

"I don't believe in curses either," said his dad, sternly. "But that's beside the point."

"Please Dad," said Peter. "Just until she gets on her feet."

The witchwoman noted the hesitation in Mark Wilson's eyes. She turned towards Peter and put a hand on his shoulder.

"Don't press your father," she said. "And don't worry about me. I'll be fine."

"But where will you sleep?"

"There's always the back of the van."

"Nonsense," said Mark Wilson, finally making up his mind. "Mrs McNab works for me, I don't work for her. And if the alternative's the back of a van, then of course you must come home with us."

25

Morag slipped in and out of sleep, living and re-living the hell of the previous night. The Bogle erupting from the ground like a tornado, whirling towards her, enveloping her in its choking fumes. Mist but not mist. Smoke but not smoke. Sliding down her throat, insinuating itself into her stomach like a parasite, sucking the life out of her.

Dr Sutherland leant over his daughter, wiping the sweat away from her forehead, massaging ointment into the livid mark that pulsed in its centre.

"Come back to me, Morag," he muttered. "Wherever you are child, come back."

And Morag came back, sitting straight up in the bed, eyes staring, grasping her father in a vice-like grip and howling. Like something not quite human. Like an animal trapped in a snare.

"Don't let it get me, Daddy," she begged, shaking her head from side to side. Foam flecked the corners of her mouth. The long damp tendrils of her red hair whipped across her face. The doctor stroked them back and put his arms around her, trying to soothe her.

"There, there," he said, holding her close as he had done when she was a toddler, when she used to have the nightmares, after her mother had died. She was trembling as she had done then, her whole body alive to some unknown terror.

"Nothing's going to get you," he said fiercely, "Not while I have breath in my body."

Morag slumped against him. She had passed out again.

Dr Sutherland laid her down gently, drawing the covers over her, wondering what could have done this to her, knowing, but not wanting to know.

Mrs McNab was back to her old formidable self. White-faced with fury, all signs of her recent change of heart erased by the arrival of the unexpected guest, she stood in the library with her jaw jutting aggressively.

"If that woman comes into the house, I'm leaving," she spluttered.

Mr Wilson regarded her evenly, refusing to be riled.

"Be reasonable, Mrs McNab," he said. "Miss

McClure has nowhere else to go. She's lost everything in the fire."

"Aye well, it's the fate of all witches," said Mrs McNab, darkly. "It always ends in fire."

"Don't talk such nonsense," said Mark Wilson. He'd just about had enough for one night. "We can't very well let her sleep on the mountainside."

"I don't care where she sleeps," said Mrs McNab. "As long as it's not under the same roof as me. As for that spawn of Satan." Here she indicated Ariel who, sensing her antagonism, hissed menacingly at her. "Filthy, smelly thing," she said. "I mean it. If they come in, I'll pack my bags and go."

"I can't stop you of course, Mrs McNab," said Peter's dad. "It's only a temporary arrangement. But if you feel you can't deal with that then it's your choice."

"Well!" Mrs McNab bristled like a threatened hedgehog. "After all I've done. When I think of the hours – the extra hours without pay – looking after that mite upstairs, and this is the thanks I get."

"And don't think we're not grateful. We are, of course. I don't know what we would have done without you. I don't want you to go."

"Then send her packing."

"You know I can't do that." said Mr Wilson and then, seeing it was hopeless. "If you leave me a forwarding address, I'll make sure you get a bonus to cover what's owed you just as soon as I get another job."

"In that case, I won't hold my breath," said Mrs McNab, nastily, and she swept out with her head in the air.

Morag writhed against the smothering fog, unable to move, incapable of speech. Her lips began to mouth the words of Jeannie's spell – but no sound emerged. The sickly essence of death clogged her throat, filled her lungs. She coughed, retching some of the filthy stuff free – and tried again.

But this time her mind wouldn't work. Her memory had gone. The formula, so well re-membered a few moments ago, had vanished like a magician's rabbit. All that came out was gibberish.

Morag did something she hadn't done in years. She began to cry.

Her father watched helplessly as the tears slid from under her sleeping lids, wiped them away with his thumb, then sniffed, bringing the thumb up to his nose. Morag's tears smelled like her sweat did. Putrid. Sulphurous. As though something foul had infected her whole system. What?

The Bogle?

He pushed the thought away, furious at himself for even considering it. Then he stood up and fetched his coat. Loath as he was to leave her alone, he needed to find out what had gone on to reduce his daughter to such a state.

As he went outside to start his car, dawn was spilling into the morning sky in strands of pink and gold.

Mrs McNab was as good as her word. First thing, before even Johnny had stirred, she was packed. While the rest of the house still slept, she loaded the Volkswagen and disappeared down the drive in a cloud of smoke and bad humour. As she rounded the bend, on the wrong side of the road, she almost collided with the doctor coming in the opposite direction.

He wound down the window and stuck out his head. He looked as though he hadn't slept a wink.

"Where are you off to at this hour, Fiona?" he said.

"I've quit," said Mrs McNab. "Enough is enough. That house has a jinx on it. The mite, heaven help him, has brought the Bogle's breath in with him. It's poisoning the air."

"Don't talk daft, woman."

"Don't tell me not to talk daft. I know what I know. And to cap it all, they've brought the witchwoman into the house. Her. Who probably raised the blighted thing in the first place."

"So you'll be out of a job then?"

"What if I am?"

"You could do me a favour." Here he leant out and handed her a house key. "Morag's on her own.

She's not well. I'd be obliged if you could go and keep an eye on her."

Mrs McNab took the key reluctantly, remembering Peter's panic of the night before, the general exodus from the house, the talk of Morag being alone at Crossmaglen.

"What's wrong with her?"

"Damned if I know," said the doctor wearily. "The same thing that ails Johnny Wilson. She's got it badly and I'm worried to death. Back up and let me through, will you, Fiona? Whatever it is, I need some answers."

Morag thrashed in her crumpled bed, living through an action replay. As if once wasn't enough, the endless loop of her memory played the horror over and over. Like a broken record stuck in a groove. The stench of decay, the pain in her muscles, the feeling that something unspeakably evil was gnawing at her soft insides, eating her alive from within.

A smell of cankerous growths enveloped her. It leaked out of her pores. She was possessed by a foulness as black as burning rubber. The taste of pitch boiled in her throat. The unimaginable fear of a thousand lost souls overwhelmed her senses, turning her bones to jelly. Her brain melted at the sheer intensity of the sensation. How much terror could a person stand before going mad?

Somewhere, from a million miles away, she could

hear a car approaching. From another time, another place, she could just make out a familiar voice. It came to her through a drift of other voices. Voices trapped within her, voices pleading to be set free. Released from everlasting torment. A single voice screaming...

"Morag. Morag. Get away. Run."

Whose voice?

Peter's.

Her eyes snapped open.

Mrs McNab sat at the end of the bed, a carrion crow in a charcoal topcoat, her face grim as an undertakers.

Suddenly Morag was three years old again, this same face hanging over her, threatening her with the Bogle if she didn't go to sleep. She shrank back, burrowing her head into the damp pillow, covering her eyes with shaking hands.

The prediction had come true. Mrs McNab had been right. The Bogle had bided its time. But it had got her in the end. And no one could help her. Not her daddy. Not anyone. The Bogle had got her and she was doomed to die in agony. The one person that might have helped her had let her down. Had left her to face the monster on her own. Deserted her.

Or had he?

What if the Bogle had got him too?

She had to find out.

She sat up and faced Mrs McNab. Outfaced her.

Staring like a demented thing, demanding an answer. Mrs McNab quailed against the stare, leaning away from it, pulling the collar of her coat around her throat, as though afraid that Morag might suddenly launch herself from the other end of the bed and tear that throat out with her bare teeth.

"Peter?" Morag croaked, bloodied eyes red-raw in the dawn light. "Where's Peter?"

26

"She's been asking for you." Mrs McNab, still in her topcoat, looking as though she might not be staying, opened the door and ushered him inside.

Peter had left his father and the doctor frantically discussing, over a cup of instant coffee, the events of the previous evening and the possible causes of the mysterious malady that had laid both their children low.

Jeannie had stayed at a discreet distance, remaining in Johnny's room while the men went downstairs and argued over the various possibilities. Meningitis. Brain fever. Sleeping sickness. Even the poison spider theory put forward by Mark Wilson. At no time was the Bogle mentioned, as though neither of these two practical, modern professionals wanted to admit to the other that he thought such nonsense was a possibility.

However, both agreed that something HAD to be done. Finally, it was decided that the best, the only plan, was keep the children stable and send for an expert in psychosomatic neurology. When Peter's dad reluctantly explained his current financial situation, Dr Sutherland told him not to be "such an eejit", that you didn't think about money at a time like this and he should put that side of it right out of his head. Then they both went up to have another look at Johnny.

Standing by Morag's bedside, looking down on her flushed face, Peter's heart sank. Whatever "experts" were sent for, he knew would be a waste of time. It was down to him to do something about Morag's condition. She looked dreadful, her fingers picking at the bedclothes, her lips constantly working in her delirium. The putrescent mark, green and yellow and hideous, throbbed in the centre of her forehead. Just like Johnny's. Poor Johnny, wracked with fever, tortured by waking dreams, wasted to a shadow in the space of just a few weeks.

He couldn't, wouldn't let the same thing happen to Morag.

"What went on last night?"

Peter jumped, turned to where Mrs McNab stood at his shoulder, bright bird eyes alive with curiosity.

"You wouldn't believe me if I told you."

"Try me."

Was it his imagination, or was there a slight softening in the stern features? He knew Mrs McNab had a better nature. He'd seen it the night he and Morag had found the body in the library.

He decided to take a chance.

"We raised the Bogle," he said.

There was a sharp intake of breath from the housekeeper.

"I knew it," she said. "She's been on about it in her sleep, but I thought it might have been a nightmare. Whatever possessed you to do such a thing?"

"We thought we could outface it, get it to release Johnny. Jeannie helped. She gave us a spell and a potion and a sign to ward off evil."

He waited for Mrs McNab to laugh. She didn't. Instead, she said "Aye, that one has the power all right. If anyone could flummox the Bogle, she could. It was one of her kind let it loose in the first place."

"Anyway, now that she's been burned out, all her books have gone. She's lost all the information she needed to outfox the thing. I don't know what we'll do. I have the potion but Morag had the spell. The one won't work without the other."

As if she'd heard them, Morag began to mutter in her sleep. A rhyme. Faint but insistent. Over and over. Peter leant close to listen.

"What's she saying?" said Mrs McNab.

"It's the spell," said Peter, excitedly. "Quick, get something to write with before she stops."

Mrs McNab clattered downstairs, returning a few moments later with a biro and Dr Sutherland's prescription pad. Too late. Morag had lapsed into silence again.

Peter shook her, talking into her face, trying to bring her round, pleading, begging.

"Morag. Morag. Wake up. It's me. Peter."

"Peter."

Morag opened her eyes, eyes wide with terror at the scene that was replaying itself over and over in her head. She had remembered the spell, shouted it out, vomiting some of the choking fog out with the words. The Bogle had shifted inside her, grumbling, gurgling in her veins. But without the potion it was useless.

She shouted the spell again now, into Peter's face. Behind him, Mrs McNab began to scribble frantically.

"The potion," Morag cried, making great welts in Peter's forearms with the fierceness of her grip. "It doesn't work without the potion." Then, remembering where she was, that the damage had already been done, she sank down on to the pillows and began to weep.

"You left me," she sobbed. "You never came."

Peter, who had never thought to see Morag, of all people, cry, took her hand, helplessly.

"I didn't leave you. I was late."

"Same thing."

"I couldn't help it. I tried to get there in time. I'm sorry, Morag. I'm so sorry."

Morag sat up, grasping his shoulders, grinding her teeth in anguish. Hot tears ran down her face. A stench of bad meat, rotting fish, rose on her breath as she spoke.

"You have to help me, Peter," she said. "You have to do something about it. You've no idea what it's like. It's inside me. Eating me alive. I can feel it moving in there, like a maggot hatching eggs. I can feel all the people it's possessed before. I can feel the hangman's noose, the flames," here she screamed, throwing her head back in agony, her face contorted like the face in the book, the face of Jeannie McClure being devoured by fire.

Peter shuddered, took her in his arms, hugged her tight.

"Help me, Peter," Morag moaned into his chest. "Help me."

Then she slumped, a dead weight against him.

Peter laid her back on the soaking pillows, turned to Mrs McNab, his face white and drawn. Wordlessly she handed him the prescription pad.

"It's all there," she said. "For what it's worth."

Then she fished in the pocket of her topcoat and produced a key.

"This is the key to the cupboard in the library," she said. "The one with Mr Blane's books in it.

Give it to Jeannie McClure. The one on the Bogle should give her everything she needs."

Peter stood up, wrapped his arms around the housekeeper, squeezing her tight.

"Away with you," she said, struggling against him but not sounding too cross. "I cannae breathe."

Peter tucked the spell and the key in his trouser pocket, looked down at his comatose friend, leant forward to touch the mark, hot and spreading under his hand.

"Thanks, Mrs McNab," he said. "I hope it works."

Mrs McNab removed her topcoat and rolled up her sleeves.

"Aye, well it'll have to, won't it," she said, practically. "Now away off home with you. And not a word to your father or the doctor about this. I'm enough of a laughing stock as it is, already. And don't worry about her," she added. "I'll take good care of her."

"I know you will, Mrs McNab," said Peter and he hared down the stairs and out into the bright morning.

27

By the time Peter got back home, the doctor had gone off on his rounds, Johnny had been bathed and fed and Jeannie and his father were having breakfast at the big table.

Real breakfast. Bacon and eggs and toast and coffee. Not the porridge and kippers which they'd been presented with under Mrs McNab's regime. Peter found that he was famished and wolfed down two helpings of everything before going upstairs to slip the key and the rewritten spell into the back of the top drawer in his tallboy.

Then he went in to check on Johnny.

The little boy was sitting up, pale but quiet, with Ariel purring in his lap. Round his neck, peeping from under his pyjama top, was one of Jeannie's amulets.

"How are you?" said Peter, his spirits lifting at the obvious improvement.

Johnny smiled weakly.

"Bit better," he said. "The nice lady gave me this." Here he fingered the amulet. "She said it would keep the nightmares away."

"Then it will," said Peter.

"Are you sure?"

"Of course I'm sure," said Peter. "Look, I have one too."

Johnny heaved a great sigh of relief.

"I think I'll have a little sleep now," he said and closed his eyes.

For the first time since the night of the Bogle, his face, thin and drawn though it was, didn't contort in sleep. His mouth settled into a half-smile and his hands, resting on the fur of the big cat's back, were still.

Jeannie's power was obviously having a positive effect.

And not just on Johnny. On everything. In just one day the big, gloomy house had undergone a complete sea-change. She had taken down the curtains – except for those in the bedrooms – and opened all the windows to let in some light and air. She had filled the house with wild flowers and floated candles in bowls of rainwater. And she sang, her soft, clear voice shifting the stagnant energy, recharging the atmosphere with ancient Highland song-spells of love and good fortune.

She moved into Mrs McNab's old rooms on the

top floor and set Peter to clearing a patch of garden for her herbs outside the kitchen door. It kept him busy and took his mind off Morag for an hour or so. He once even found himself whistling along with Jeannie as her voice carried through the open window from the kitchen where she was preparing a blackberry pie and a batch of griddle scones.

The food had improved out of all recognition – rabbit stew and fresh salad as opposed to Mrs McNab's glutinous concoctions. All in all, a baleful presence seemed to have disappeared from the property. Which, of course, it had. A McClure was living under the roof again.

The other Jeannie's curse had been lifted.

If it hadn't been for Johnny, now so slight that you could almost see through him, life in the big house would have been nearly perfect. Ariel took up residence at the bottom of the little boy's bed. Like a watchdog. Or a guardian angel. And nothing anyone could do would shift him. He curled himself round the child's feet and the loud purr seemed to give Johnny comfort.

Jeannie took charge in this department too. Not ham-fistedly like Mrs McNab would have done, but gently, gradually, soothing Johnny's fears, treating him to the kind of tender, loving care he hadn't had since his mother died. She began by making up a warm poultice of linen saturated with camomile to bathe his head. It seemed to relax him so that when, a few hours later, she brought up a herb tisane and a small silver spoon with which to administer it, he didn't object or spit it out but swallowed it like a lamb.

Peter observed that his mum had worked along similar lines, getting her way quietly without fuss. And his father looked less strained than he had done in a very long time. He set up his lap-top by Johnny's bedside and spent the next few hours writing letters to the various oil companies, saying he was unexpectedly available. But as luck (or maybe Jeannie's intervention with some higher powers?) would have it, before he had even time to post them, a call came, offering him an interview in Aberdeen the next day.

Peter hadn't had a chance to discuss the issue of the Bogle with Jeannie since Morag had been "taken". It had been hard for him to be patient. His visit to his friend in the morning had been harrowing in the extreme. Although she calmed a little when he went back that evening and gave her his amulet for protection. She had lost hers somewhere at Crossmaglen.

The doctor, who had come in and caught Peter clasping it round her neck had, at first, been adamant that Morag shouldn't wear it.

"Superstitious rubbish," he had called it.

It was Mrs McNab, who had finally taken her coat off and was now firmly ensconced in the Sutherland household, who persuaded him otherwise.

"Whatever gets her through the night," she had said, sternly. "Do you want the lassie to be happy? Or do you want to prove a point?"

And the doctor had retired, grumbling, to his study.

So it was next morning, with Mark Wilson safely off the premises on the way to his interview, before Peter was able to give Jeannie the key to the cupboard. The witchwoman took it with a surprised smile.

"Fiona McNab, doing something for me," she said. "Wonders will never cease."

Sure enough, as Mrs McNab had predicted, she found what she needed to raise the Bogle again in Hunter S. Blane's book "Ancient Beliefs – The Origin of the Monster".

Peter heaved a sigh of relief.

"I don't think Morag could last till next dark of the moon," he said. "The sooner we get on with it the better."

"Just as well I persuaded your father to stay in Aberdeen overnight," said Jeannie. "I told him that even if he gets this job he should see as many people as he can while he's up there. We have thirty-six hours before he gets back. It's not nearly long enough, but it'll have to do."

28

Peter and the witchwoman sat at the table, Hunter S. Blane's book open at the section on "bringing the Bogle to heel". The ritual was a complicated one and Jeannie was thankful she hadn't had to try to reconstruct it from memory.

Also in front of them were the original potion and the rewritten spell.

Jeannie picked up the small phial of clear liquid and cradled it in the palm of her hand.

"It will have lost some of its efficacy but I am pretty sure I can re-empower it," she said. "The spell will have to be redrawn again too. I will do that tonight. Upstairs. In my rooms. Alone." She looked at Peter hard. "Whatever you hear, you must promise me not to come up. Is that clear?"

"It's not dangerous, is it?" said Peter, nervously.

"Not if you stay out of it, it isn't," said Jeannie. "But I would be lying to you if I said that these are not powerful forces that I'm calling upon."

"What kind of forces?" Peter had visions of the Prince of Darkness himself materializing in the attic. He shivered. A couple of months ago, safe in the urban normality of Hampstead, he would have laughed such an idea to scorn. But that was before he met the Bogle.

The witchwoman took in Peter's worried expression and laid a hand on his arm.

"If it's any consolation," she said. "They are forces of light. The white must aye counteract the black. And the Bogle is black as sin. But they are forces nonetheless. They must be harnessed. I cannot be distracted. You must not come in."

"I won't," Peter promised.

"Luckily, I have the van," she went on, thinking ahead, "so we don't have a transport problem."

"So you'll be coming too?" Peter was much relieved.

"I will," said Jeannie, "this time we cannae leave anything to chance. But I will only be there for support. I cannae do it for you. Do you remember the sign?"

"I think so."

"Show me."

Peter made the sign to ward off evil, curling his left forefinger round to touch the thumb lightly, placing the right-hand palm in front of the aperture and holding the whole across his face to shield his eyes.

"Good," said the witchwoman. "But I must draw the pentacle again," and she did just that, using one of Johnny's red markers."

"Wait a minute," said Peter, observing her handiwork when she had finished, recalling how she'd drawn the same sign on Morag's hand. Much good it had done her. "We have a problem. A BIG problem."

"And that is?"

"Well, Dad's not here so we can get Johnny out of the house, easily. But what about the doctor? He's hardly going to sit back and let me take Morag out to face the Bogle. Especially not in your van."

Jeannie cradled her face in her hands and thought for a bit.

"I will need to make up a sleeping draught," she said, eventually. "And Mrs McNab will need to slip it into his cocoa. I wouldn't normally do such a thing. But desperate times call for desperate measures."

She stood up from the table. Peter was tall for his age but she still stood eye to eye with him.

"Now I must get to work," she said, fixing him with her cool, grey gaze. "And I need your solemn word. That you will stay with Johnny. And that whatever you hear during the time I'm upstairs you won't come in. Promise?"

"Promise."

Many times during the long night that followed, Peter was to regret that promise. Huddled by Johnny's bedside, trying to close his ears against the thumps and howls filtering down from the top floor, more than once he was tempted to rush upstairs and fling open the door.

But he kept his word.

He stayed put.

Ariel, however, deserted his post, retreating to the attic rooms to assist his mistress. Whatever unnamed and unnameable rituals she was engaged in that produced such unearthly noises, such fierce flashes of fiery light, clearly the cat played an important part.

Next morning they both emerged into the cold, grey light of dawn, exhausted and bedraggled. Peter, waking from a nightmare of being lost in a sulphurous fog, looked up blearily.

The witchwoman held out the glass phial, the liquid turned once again to azure blue. Then she handed him a paper identical to the one which Morag had crumpled so carelessly into the pocket of her shorts.

"Take them," she said. "It is done."

Peter looked down at the spell and the potion. He was torn between relief and sheer unadulterated terror. They were ready to face the enemy, once again.

With one distinct difference.

This time, he was on his own.

29

"Hello, Mrs McNab."

Peter stood at the doorway, sweating. A cloying heat had descended with the darkness at the end of an endless day during which Jeannie had made final preparations, retrieving her crystal from the ashes of her burnt-out cottage, scouring the house for various other items, all of which she had secreted in a sack in the back of the van, while Peter had kept Johnny happy – or attempted to – and tried not to think of what lay ahead.

The boy was asleep now and Peter had set off into a warm, dark evening, heavy with menace, to carry out the second part of "Operation Bogle".

More like *Mission Impossible* he had thought to himself as he pedalled through the gloom. The bike ride had left him lathered like a racehorse. He'd spent most of it looking over his shoulder. Now he had a crick in his neck.

"You should have called before you came over," Mrs McNab ushered him inside, closing the door behind him. "She's fast asleep and I won't have you disturbing her at this hour?"

"That's what I need to talk to you about," said Peter. "Is the doctor in?"

"He's had a call out but I'm expecting him home anytime. Why?"

So Peter explained the plan, swearing her to silence, finally handing over the sleeping draught, asking her, "Will you do it?"

Mrs McNab took the folded paper containing the white powder reluctantly.

"It willnac harm him, will it?"

"Jeannie says not."

"How long will it last?"

"Twelve hours at least," said Peter. "By the time he comes round it should be all over."

"I hope so." Mrs McNab nodded towards the upstairs bedroom. "She's had a terrible day. The worst one yet. Screaming and crying. Scratching herself with her nails, trying to "get it out". We've had to put gloves on her. The doctor's at the end of his tether."

Peter headed for the stairs.

"I'll go see her," he said.

Mrs McNab put out a hand to stop him.

"Leave her be." she said, firmly. "She needs the

sleep. If she comes round, I'll warn her that you'll be coming." Once again she looked at the packet of powder in her hand. "What time do you want me to..."

"Eleven o'clock should be time enough," said Peter. "It's fast acting. Call when he's asleep. We'll come straight over to pick her up."

"He likes a drop of whisky when he comes in these days," said Mrs McNab. "Soothes his nerves. I'll put it in that."

She showed Peter to the door.

"But that's as far as I'm going, mind," she added. "If you're messing about with the powers of darkness, you'll not see me outside these four walls tonight for all the tea in china."

The call came through at eleven–fifteen, the housekeeper's voice crackling with static over the line.

"All clear," she said. "He's out for the count."

Peter and the witchwoman looked at each other, Peter trying to keep the fear out of his eyes, Jeannie calm under stress, strong and somehow terrible in her control.

"Ready?" she said.

"Ready as I'll ever be."

The witchwoman bowed, smiling, swinging her arm across her body, ushering him out.

"Then let's go," she said. "It's now or never."

They were at the doctor's in under ten minutes, Johnny fast asleep in the back, Jeannie keeping the engine running while Peter took the stairs two at a time.

Morag was still asleep, which was a blessing, her pyjamas saturated with sweat, the points of her elbows and collar bone protruding through emaciated flesh that had taken on the grey-green tinge of the terminally ill. As he picked her up, Peter noticed with horror that her wonderful red hair had started to come out in clumps. A handful of it remained on the pillow like the memory of a memory as he gathered her up in his arms.

She whimpered but didn't stir as he carried her downstairs, past the housekeeper, past the dark sitting-room where Dr Sutherland sat slumped in his armchair, snoring gently. Mrs McNab had covered him with a blanket. She raised a hand in farewell as Peter rushed past, whispering "good luck" to his retreating back and then, as she shut the door behind him and locked it again, "Rather you than me."

Morag came round briefly as Peter tucked her in beside Johnny. Jeannie had placed a couple of lilos in the back, covered in rugs and cushions, to make the journey as comfortable as possible.

"Where are we going?" she said, blearily.

"Never mind," Peter stroked her forehead. "Go back to sleep."

"What time is it?" she asked, before slipping back into unconsciousness.

"Eleven-thirty," said Peter, grimly.

And then they were out of there, headed for the crossroads at Crossmaglen and whatever fate awaited them.

It was countdown time. And for good or ill, the final conflict was about to take place.

30

An ominous silence hung over the crossroads when they got to Crossmaglen.

The heat had turned the valley into a furnace in which every inhalation of breath required a superhuman effort. A smell of rotten eggs hung in the stagnant air. The atmosphere felt heavy enough to break glass. It was like driving through glue.

Jeannie parked the van as close as she could to the big standing stone, then went round the back to open the doors.

"You take Morag," she said. "I'll see to Johnny."

Peter did as he was bid. As he lifted her out, Morag opened he eyes and came to.

"Where are we?" she said, groggily. "What's happening?"

Peter sat her gently on the grass, her back propped against the monolith.

"At Crossmaglen," he said. "We've come to finish this thing once and for all."

Morag began to wail. Peter clamped a hand over her mouth to nip her hysteria in the bud.

"Shhhh," he said. "Don't be scared. It'll be all right. I promise you."

He stared steadily into the green eyes, hoping he looked more sure of the outcome than he was. Then, appealing to her better nature, he said, "I need you to be strong. For just a little while more. For Johnny's sake. Someone has to look out for him while Jeannie and I do what has to be done. Can you manage that?"

Morag nodded wordlessly.

"If I take my hand away, do you promise not to scream or do anything silly?"

Again, Morag nodded.

Peter removed his hand.

"The spell?" Morag said, desperately. "I can't remember it."

Peter patted his back pocket.

"It's here," he reassured her. "Don't worry. You don't have to do anything. I've got it all under control."

Morag flung her arms round his neck, burying her face in his chest. Her shoulders shook but she made no sound.

Peter detached her gently, looked into a face tight with suppressed terror.

"OK?"

"OK," quavered Morag. "But be careful."

"You can bet on it."

He nodded to the witchwoman, standing beside them holding Johnny in her arms. Without a word she laid the little boy in Morag's lap.

" 'Lo Morag," he said, weakly.

Morag wrapped her arms round him.

"Hey there," she said then, looking up at Peter. "I'm all right now. Get on with it."

As he moved away, Peter couldn't help thinking that the two pathetic figures huddled by the base of the basalt pillar looked like nothing more than a pair of human sacrifices waiting to be devoured by some bestial deity. The marks on their foreheads stood out like ritual tattoos. They were as thin as living skeletons.

The witchwoman, meanwhile, was busying herself with a sack, which she took out of the front seat of the van. Removing the contents, one item at a time, she laid each out with careful precision.

Her crystal, its clarity somewhat dimmed by its recent ordeal by fire, she set aside on a raised hummock of heather. Round Morag and Johnny, at the four points of the compass, she placed an old silver goblet, a magician's wand, a wrought-iron pot stand in the shape of a pentacle, and a huge double-edged claymore, weapon of the clans, man-height and almost as heavy as herself.

The four protective symbols of the ancient power of the Tarot.

Then, with a thumbs up sign at Peter, she retired halfway up the hill and sat down cross-legged, the crystal in her lap and Ariel by her side.

None of them spoke. There was nothing to say. Two minutes they waited. Two long, long minutes. And then the church bell chimed down in the valley.

Midnight was upon them.

Peter straightened up, spell in one hand, potion in the other. His guts were in a turmoil but otherwise he felt strangely calm.

There was a sudden total absence of sound. A silence so thick you could cut it with a knife.

Then the van began to shudder, as though shaken by an invisible hand, and Ariel began to yowl. One by one all four tyres exploded sending strips of scorched rubber into the air. The van fell to the ground with a thump and was still. Johnny started to cry, small mewling hiccups of sound.

The cold came down with an icy rush as the Bogle surged up from the ground. An ominous grey column of smoke, swirling, questing. The stench was unbearable. Peter put his hand across his nose and mouth to try to keep it out. Morag was coughing now, Johnny crying in earnest.

Above and to his left, Peter heard the witchwoman gasp. He, himself was struck dumb, the bottom dropping out of his stomach. This was how Morag must have felt, he thought. Overwhelmed at what had confronted her. All on her own.

The Bogle had grown to gigantic proportions. It hung over the standing stone like a mini-skyscraper, its shadow falling across the cowering children. For a breath-held moment it remained motionless, suspended in time and space. Then it attacked, swooping down towards Peter. A Japanese killer-wave. Terrifying. Unstoppable.

And in that instant, Peter knew that neither spell nor potion nor secret sign would hold this monster in its present form. It had grown too strong.

Panic overtook him.

His only chance now was to run. Get away. Save himself.

He turned on his heel. He had to get out of there. There was no way he could beat this thing alone. He was only human. And the Bogle was...

His foot skidded on something. A piece of rubber from one of the tyres. He lost his balance and fell on his knees. He could feel the Bogle's rancid breath on the back of his head, ruffling his hair.

"Up." Jeannie's voice. Strong. Decisive. "Get up, Peter."

He turned his head towards the sound.

The witchwoman was standing now, arms and legs outstretched, sparks flashing fire from her fingertips, holding the monster at bay.

Peter tried to scramble up. He could hear the Bogle grunting above him. With all the willpower at his command, he dragged himself to his feet and turned to face the enemy.

Through the descending curtain of smothering mist he could just make out Morag's face, waxy and pale, reproaching him silently. And Johnny. Depending on him.

Then the Bogle was over and around him, insinuating itself into his nostrils, forcing itself down his thoat. He was trapped in the foul heart of the thing. Lost. No way to escape. Desperately he spat the filthy stuff out, brought the paper up to his eyes, cleared his throat and began to read.

He spoke the words loud and clear, as Jeannie had instructed, keeping his eyes fixed firmly on the text so as not to miss a syllable. The spell flooded out into the night, stirring the glutinous air, cutting through the density of the evil.

The Bogle shuddered, pulling back in surprise. It retrenched, pulsing over the standing stone. Then it started to swirl, faster and faster, sucking up energy like a tornado from the pathetic scraps of flesh that crouched, shivering, in its shadow.

Morag screamed as if she were being pulled inside out. Johnny clung to her, moaning.

Peter, jolted by the noise, raised his voice louder.

The chant began to take on a power of its own, rolling round the peaks, echoing into the crevices. The acoustics of the great natural amphitheatre, created in the time before time, by forces of nature greater than anything man could ever devise, hurled the spell up into the atmosphere so that the very heavens reverberated with the sound.

And with each phrase, each line, the Bogle, snarling in disbelief and fury, became more disempowered. It slowed to a halt, retreated backwards, shrank, its circumference imploding into its heart centre. Even that centre became less dense as the spell progressed. So that when Peter at last looked up, flinging aside the paper and unstoppering the cork from the potion, the frightful shape was much diminished. It hung suspended now, not immediately above Morag and Johnny, but several metres away. Areas of light were beginning to appear in the opaqueness, giving it an aspect of mildewed lace. From these cracks emerged the piteous wails of the damned.

Remembering the witchwoman's instructions to get as close as possible, Peter took a deep breath and, gathering all the courage he could muster, moved towards the monster. One step. Two. Three.

Then he drew back his hand and flung the contents of the bottle up and forward with all his strength.

The liquid enveloped the Bogle in a shower of spray.

The effect was immediate. The potion seemed to act like sulphuric acid. The spectre began to fizzle and foam, steam rising into the night air on the hissing howl that accompanied it. A howl of terminal agony.

The liquid ate away at the foulness, devouring

ever-expanding sections of the Bogle's essence, moving inexorably outwards, unstoppable as a plague. Like the witch in *The Wizard of Oz*, the Bogle shrank, its wonderful wickedness melting into the heather.

But the thing was not dead yet.

Its howl turned to a hate-charged shriek as it launched its tattered remains at Peter. Tentacles of mist stretched out to press him into its suppurating centre, reaching towards the tender vulnerability of his open eyes.

But thanks to the witchwoman, Peter still had the ace up his sleeve. Instead of retreating, he stepped forward, placing himself between what was left of the monster and the defenceless bodies on the ground. He raised his hands across his face, curling his left thumb and forefinger into the shape of an eye which he held up to protect his own, raising his right hand to cover the opening, the palm facing towards his attacker.

For the Bogle, it was the last straw. Brought up short, half a metre away from its intended victim – so near and yet so far – it squealed like a poisoned rat and, slithering to the ground, began to writhe in its death-throes.

But now something else was happening. From in and around the standing stone, gushes of flame and steam began to shoot up like fireworks. And with them came noises. Growling and chattering. As though a thousand dog-headed monkeys were trying to escape from the bowels of the earth. Or the pits of Hell.

Things began to appear, monstrous, malformed things, mishapen and repugnant. Vomited out of the heart of darkness. They began to hop or crawl or slither outwards from the crossroads into the surrounding undergrowth.

Suddenly, a wild figure came leaping down the hill like a gazelle, a huge ginger cat hot on its heels.

"The souls of the damned," it yelled. "The Bogle is dead, but now they are free."

And Jeannie McClure, guardian of the good, latest incarnation of an unbroken line of white witches, rushed into the centre of the crossroads to do battle. Her entire body was haloed in a faint glow of purest golden energy. As though all the powers of the Light were concentrating themselves in her. Using her as a living, breathing weapon against the Darkness.

Peter was busy with troubles of his own, swatting uselessly at a gaggle of wraith-like forms which, translucent as sun-starved jellyfish from the ocean depths, swarmed around his head. They swirled in and out, leering, grasping. He ducked each time the creatures darted in to attack, plucking at his hair, stinging like scorpions. The holding sign seemed to have little power against them. But he stood his ground. A human shield for Morag and Johnny. A king lion guarding his pride.

The witchwoman strode to his side, reached down and, with a yell that would have done

Boadicea proud, snatched the huge, double-edged sword up from the ground.

"Get the children out of here," she yelled. "Quickly. Now."

Peter didn't argue. Flinging Johnny over his shoulder in a fireman's lift, he half-carried, half-dragged Morag up the hill away from the triangle of grass. Away from danger.

The glow surrounding Jeannie McClure became brighter, more intense. As she whirled the giant claymore around her head, a weapon that by any normal standards would have been far too heavy for her to even lift, it seemed that gouts of fire leapt from her fingers. Her long, black hair stood out from her head like wire and her eyes burned with an internal flame. Her ancient crystal, halfway up the ridge where she'd dropped it, took on the glow of a full moon. A hum like a swarm of bees came from its centre and travelled along the ground, stirring the rocks of the valley floor, shaking the great standing stone to its very foundations.

With a final, guttural shout, the witchwoman raised the great sword high above her head and brought it down in a perfect arc, towards the monolith. The point caught the topmost tip square in the centre. The stone shuddered, then shuddered again. A jagged rent appeared down its length, running from root to apex. Then the whole thing burst like a boil, hurling fragments of molten basalt out into the night.

The explosion rocked the surrounding mountains, sending seismic shock-waves spiralling out into the High Hills and almost toppling Drumnadrochit's church steeple. And in Edinburgh that night, an earthquake, equivalent to six-point-five on the Richter scale, was recorded on the computers at the Centre for Geological Studies.

When the smoke cleared and the ringing in his ears had subsided, Peter looked down on a scene of utter devastation. It was as though a bomb had dropped. The land round the crossroads was bare of vegetation, the earth blackened and blighted. Of the Bogle itself nothing but a few wisps of lingering mist remained.

As he watched even these fizzled away and were swallowed into the Highland dust.

He turned and hugged Morag who hugged him back. Johnny, on the ground, wrapped himself round their ankles and hugged them both.

Then Peter held his friend away at arm's length.

"It's gone," he shouted. "The mark's gone."

Morag touched her forehead, started to laugh, stooped to stand Johnny up on his feet. The little boy, eyes clear, face unmarked, grinned up at her. Then together, hand in hand, the three of them made their weary way down the hill to where the witchwoman stood slumped in the centre of the crossroads.

The double-edged claymore drooped in her hands. The glow of power, drained by the superhuman effort she had made, had disappeared. She looked tired and drawn. With the faithful Ariel padding at her heels, she moved over to stand beside the small cairn of shattered stones, all that remained of the great rent monolith.

"The gateway is closed," she said, and then, turning to Peter, "and the Bogle is dead."

Beside her, Johnny pulled at her skirt.

"Don't be silly, Jeannie," he said. "There's no such thing as the Bogle. It's just a fairy tale invented to stop children from misbehaving themselves."

As the laughter died down, the little boy rubbed his stomach.

"I'm starving," he said. "Is it dinnertime yet? I couldn't half do with a hamburger."

Epilogue

It was amazing how quickly things got back to normal.

Dr Sutherland woke next morning to find his daughter fast asleep and apparently in the best of health. Thin but sound and with an appetite that would have done justice to a hungry horse. Of the insidious mark there was not a trace, and since Mrs McNab assured him that it had simply disappeared in the night, he didn't press the matter. He was just pleased to have her back.

The first thing he did was to call the expected specialist and tell him he wouldn't be needed after all. A "spontaneous remission" was how he put it. Then he rang the big house to see how Johnny was getting on.

"It's unbelievable," Mark Wilson told him down the phone. "I was just going to ring you. I got back in the early hours and went straight to bed. I've just come to. This morning it's as if he never had that damn mark. He's at the table now, on his fourth bowl of cornflakes, looking as right as rain."

"Aye, well, sometimes these things just clear up by themselves," said the doctor. "We should be grateful for that I suppose. I'll be round some time this afternoon to give him a check-up."

Morag was round before that. After a breakfast of bacon, eggs, sausages, tomatoes, baked beans, black pudding, mushrooms and fried bread (which she cooked herself, leaving Mrs McNab to cope with the dishes), she was off on her bicycle to see Peter.

She found him at the table in the big flagstone kitchen with Johnny, his dad, Jeannie McClure and Ariel. Mark Wilson was in high spirits, not only from the unexpected recovery of his son but with news of a successful interview and a fresh job under his belt.

Morag said she wouldn't join them thanks, she'd already had her breakfast, but oh well, if they insisted, she could murder a couple of slices of toast and jam. And she did.

Mr Wilson was off to Aberdeen and his new job later in the day and the witchwoman was to stay on as a permanent house guest. From the way Peter's dad was looking at her, Morag thought that it wouldn't be long before Jeannie might be joining the household in a more official capacity.

"Your daddy seems very taken with Jeannie," she said, as they pedalled off up the glen, stopping every now and then to let Johnny catch up. They were off on a picnic which the witchwoman had put up for them. Ham and pickle sandwiches on home-made bread, big wodges of fresh apple pie and a flask full of lemonade.

"You've got to admit she's an improvement on Mrs McNab," grinned Peter.

"No question," said Morag, glumly. "It looks as though I'm lumbered with her now."

"Oh, she's not a bad old stick," said Peter. "As long as you don't have to put up with her cooking. And at least she won't be able to threaten you with the Bogle any more."

They were all feeling in fine form. The sun was shining, the birds were singing and it had been settled over breakfast that Peter would be going to the co-ed academy with Morag at the beginning of September.

Johnny would join the junior section of the big school – the buildings were next door to each other and shared a playground – so they'd all be able to travel on the same bus together and Peter could keep an eye on his little brother until he settled in.

Life looked good.

The destruction of the standing stone and the devastation around Crossmaglen was put down to a freak of nature – an explosion of natural gases. Even though Fiona McNab continued to tap her nose and purse her lips, nobody really took much notice of her.

So all was well that ended well.

Or was it?

A couple of months later an American family, six in all, halted in the middle of the mountains to get their bearings. They were on their way to the Highland games at Braemar, their main object to get a picture of the queen in her kilt with which to amaze all their friends back in Sugarland, Texas. Since it was their first visit to Bonnie Scotland, they had decided to travel by the scenic route.

Now they were lost.

As Mrs Van Outen pored over the crumpled map with the aid of a torch, for it was pitch-black outside the camper, the four children argued and grizzled in the back.

"I can't find anything that says Drum-na-whatever-it-is," she said plaintively.

"Give it here," said her husband, snatching the map away from her. "I swear, Marlene, you couldn't find your way out of a paper bag." He turned and bellowed over his shoulder, "And will you kids pipe down? You're like to drive me demented. Maybe you'd rather get out and walk the rest of the way?"

A sullen silence descended on the camper. The head of the family sighed heavily and turned the map the right way up.

"This is it right here," he said, jabbing a stubby forefinger at a point where three roads converged.

"Crossmaglen crossroads. Drum-na-whatsit is just over the next hill."

Marlene Van Outen pulled her voluminous Arran cardigan – bought in a tourist shop on Edinburgh's Prince's Street – closer round her voluminous frame. Outside the camper a sudden fog had descended, completely blanking out the road ahead.

"Say, honey," she said. "Does it suddenly feel awfully cold to you?"

It was two minutes to midnight – and dark of the moon.

THE BOGLE

Johnny tried to cry out to the others to wait. But he hadn't enough breath for it. He could hear the soft keening whoosh of the Bogle coming closer. The stench of its foulness made him retch. He began to whimper to himself, trying to wake himself up as he had on the previous evenings.

But this was no dream.

This was desperately, horrifyingly real.

And then suddenly, his front wheel hit a particularly deep rut and he catapulted headfirst into the road.

Just before his head thudded into the rock that knocked him senseless, he had a brief, vivid image of his mother's face smiling up at him.

Then all was darkness.

Have you read?

Point Horror
Unleashed

THE BOGLE

Samantha Lee

SCHOLASTIC

Scholastic Children's Books,
Commonwealth House, 1-19 New Oxford Street,
London WC1A 1NU, UK
a division of Scholastic Ltd
London ~ New York ~ Toronto ~ Sydney ~ Auckland
Mexico City ~ New Delhi ~ Hong Kong

First published in the UK by Scholastic Ltd, 2000

Copyright © Samantha Lee, 2000

ISBN 0 439 01485 9

Typeset by
Cambrian Typesetters, Frimley, Camberley, Surrey
Printed by Cox and Wyman Ltd, Reading, Berks.

10 9 8 7 6 5 4 3 2 1